No Doubles Defense (Tag & Skye Part 2)

A Columbia Gems Baseball Romance

MJ Compton

Comptonplations Publishing

NO DOUBLES DEFENSE (Tag & Skye Part 2)

2nd edition

Originally published in 2017 as MASK OF THE KING

Editor: Rebecca Fairfax

Cover Art: 100 Covers

Published in the United States of America by

Comptonplations Publishing

EBOOK ISBN: 978-1-959923-07-7

PRINT ISBN: 978-1-959923-08-4

www.comptonplations.com

NO DOUBLES DEFENSE (TAG & SKYE PART 2)

DEDICATION, ACKNOWLEDGEMENT, AUTHOR NOTE

DEDICATION:

As always, to Steve.

ACKNOWLEDGEMENTS:

To the Purple Hazers: Christine Wenger, Carol Lombardo, Kris Fletcher, and Gayle Callen. You keep me propped at my desk when I want to surrender, and that's the best thing an author's friends can do.

Matthew Healy: water cooler brainstorming is best!

BFA Morning Office Participants. You keep me going!

AUTHOR NOTE:

Since this story was originally written, the rules of baseball have changed. Any errors are my own.

Contents

Wednesday, February 22 – Krewe of Druids Parade

Tucker Alexander Gentry—Tag to the baseball world—rented a red sports car at Armstrong International Airport and plugged the address his former teammate had provided into his phone.

God it felt good to be out of the wheelchair and independently mobile. Weeks without being able to walk, much less drive, were behind him. He still faced months of physical therapy, though. His last visit with the team doctor had sucked. Prognosis: Tag would miss the whole upcoming season.

If he ever got his hands on that punk from New York... The league could fine the little bastard who had plowed cleats-first into Tag's leg all they wanted, suspend the son of a bitch for a couple of games, or ban him for life like Shoeless Joe or Pete Rose. Didn't matter. No disciplinary action could give Tag back the World Series he'd missed. That theft burned worse than missing the spring training currently in session or sitting out the entire upcoming season.

So when Noah Nash, former pitching great for the Columbia Gems, had invited Tag to New Orleans for Mardi Gras, Tag had jumped at the chance. Figuratively.

Tag concentrated on the unfamiliar traffic patterns instead of on what the hell he was going to do if he couldn't play baseball again. Noah had said he might have something for him. There were only so many broadcasting positions, only so many coaching and scouting jobs—but hundreds of retired players. Pathetic men who were lost without a stadium or team to define them. Tag vowed he would never join their ranks.

The rest of the Gems were at spring training while Tag had been stuck in Columbia. Stuck and feeling sorry for himself. He should have been in Florida with the rest of the guys. Red was.

And if he couldn't be with his team, he ought to be able to do something else. Bungee jumping. Cave diving. *Something.* He was climbing the walls when he should have been rock climbing. Except his contract prevented him from doing anything that might endanger his rehab. If Terra, his currently off-again girlfriend, had been around, she could have amused him. But Terra was waiting for some volcano on some Pacific island to erupt. And they were off again. Probably permanently.

And Red? She was his new best friend. Who came with benefits. Came with— He could list a hundred ways she came and a hundred more ways he wanted to try. But Red was the team caterer and had been summoned to spring training along with the rest of the Gems.

So Noah's hint of a future career only sweetened the New Orleans vacation concept.

Once Tag got off the highway and into the city improper—and New Orleans in February was definitely improper—he ran into traffic issues. Although Fat Tuesday wasn't for another six days, the frenzied city throbbed with its Carnival celebration. Parades closed blocks of some streets the phone app told him to use. Costumed pedestrians clustered in inconvenient spots, where automobiles became intruders and had to yield to the citizens and tourists.

Everyone looked as if they were having a good time, something Tag hadn't experienced in too long. Except for some increasingly rare interludes with Red.

Red. Celeste "Skye" Schuyler. Owner of Skye's the Limit Catering. Damn it, he was trying not to think about her. The team had hired her to feed him while he'd been laid up. Once his cast had come off, she'd no longer made house calls. And with the cessation of house calls came the end of booty calls.

Tag missed her. He was loath to admit it, even to himself, but he'd grown fond of their sparring. All the things he'd ever heard about feisty redheads were true. At least, in her case. Just thinking about her had his cock twitching.

Tag finally gave up trying to follow directions and called Noah. "Just stay on the line with me and tell me how to get to your place from where I am."

Another half hour passed before Tag found the street in the French Quarter.

"You should have taken a cab," Noah said.

"You should have suggested that before I got here," Tag replied.

They were settled in Noah's high-ceilinged den with drinks in their hands. The smooth whiskey relaxed Tag. Damn, he needed this. He hadn't known how tense he was. The way life had been conspiring against him had done things to his insides he hadn't known about until now.

"How are you liking life in the slow lane?" Noah asked.

"I'm not." The ice in Tag's glass rattled as he brought it to his mouth.

"Retirement takes getting used to."

"I'm not retired. I'm on the disabled list." Maybe he was swallowing his bourbon too quickly, because the muscles in his throat felt as if they were rebelling.

Noah snickered. "According to the press, Crabtree did such a number on your leg you'll never play again. You couldn't even get a spot on an American League team as DH."

Tag's fingers tightened on his glass. "I wouldn't believe everything I read—oh I forgot. You can't read."

"I can hear just fine," Noah shot back. "All the sports networks are saying—"

"My batting average might not be good enough to be a designated hitter, but for a catcher, I'm damned good with the bat." The sports networks didn't know shit. HIPAA laws kept his medical issues private.

"You keep telling yourself that."

"Positive attitude is everything." Or so Red kept telling him. If it helped him get back in the game, he would repeat the affirmation hourly. Red believed in that shit. All he knew was it couldn't hurt.

"How are you going to catch with your knee messed up?"

That was a problem. Crouching behind home plate for nine innings strained a guy's knees and thighs. In addition to breaking his tibia, Crabtree's cleats had sneaked behind Tag's leg guards to the vulnerable back of the knee. Torn a bunch of muscles and nerves. But people had their tendons, ligaments, and cartilage repaired all the time. No biggie. He could come back. Better than ever. So what if he'd lost sensation in the skin of his calf? Didn't need to feel mosquito bites to play ball.

"I'll manage. Thanks for your concern." Tag couldn't keep the sarcasm out of his voice.

"And you're getting old."

Since when was thirty-five old? It was past time to change the subject. "What are you doing these days?"

Noah took another swallow of his drink. Flashed a look of discomfort. Maybe embarrassment. "Favors."

Unless hell had frozen over or there was something in it for him. Noah Nash didn't do favors.

"For anyone interesting?" Tag asked.

Noah shrugged. "I know a lot of people. People need things."

Informative answer. "When you called me, you said something about—"

"Let's not talk business." Noah swallowed more bourbon. "You're here to party, right? After being laid up all winter?"

"You got that right." Mardi Gras in the French Quarter. A new experience. He'd been in spring training every February since he was eighteen. He had a lot of catching up to do.

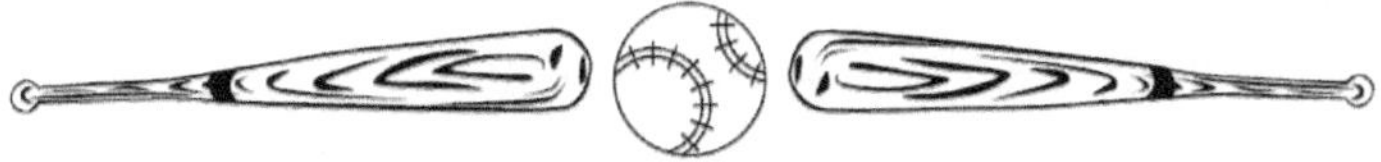

"He didn't say how pretty you are."

The man who answered the door was handsome in a rundown sort of way. A barely noticeable paunch. Bloodshot eyes. Whiskey on his breath.

"I think I have the wrong address." Celeste "Skye" Schuyler tightened her grip on her suitcase and turned to head back to the taxi lingering at the curb. She'd asked the driver to wait. Just in case. Her intuition was working overtime.

"You're Skye of Skye's the Limit," the man said. "You cater for the Gems. I'm a former Gem."

She had hated being in Florida for spring training but wasn't sure New Orleans during Carnival was a better situation. Until she had a signed contract with the Columbia Gems baseball organization, she needed to cater to their whims in addition to catering their meals. If that meant working a weeklong Mardi Gras house party in New Orleans for a former Gems' star pitcher, she'd do it. Even if it felt wrong.

"You're Noah Nash?" she asked.

"Yes. Come on in. I'm real sorry for the last-minute request, but that's the kind of guy I am. I decided to have a house party, and of course every caterer in the state has been booked for months. Then I heard about you."

Maybe he was trying to be affable, but nothing he said rang true. She waved at the cab driver. Apparently she was in the right place.

Until she had her signed contract from the team, she was at the mercy of whoever wanted to hire her. Including washed-up baseball players.

"Hey Tag!" he called. "Guess who's here?"

Tag? Here?

Not good. Tag Gentry was a big part of the reason she'd agreed to go to spring training in Florida.

Sure enough, the familiar shape, the face she was entirely too fond of limped into the wide center hall. He was using his cane. She'd bought him that cane. Had ordered the black matte finish pinstriped in Gem teal.

"Red?" He sounded as happy to see her as she was to see him.

Or maybe she was projecting. Wishing she wasn't so relieved he was in New Orleans. She mentally scolded her fingers for wanting to ruffle his dark, almost curly hair.

Play it cool. There was no way of telling whether or not Nash knew about her relationship with Tag. After all, she and Tag were friends. Only friends. And occasional sex partners. Fuck buddies. "Tag. Nice to see you again."

He nodded. The aloofness in his gray eyes told her how he wanted to play it. Distant acquaintances. She had no problem with that. Because that was the way their relationship should be.

"Let me show you to your room," Nash said. He took her suitcase from her. "There's a guesthouse out back. I figured you girls would want your privacy."

Nash opened a door at the other end of the wide center hall and led the way into a courtyard. Skye had to stop. Even though it was February, flowering trees lit up the landscape with splashes of color, as if celebrating their own version of Mardi Gras.

Nash unlocked the door and stepped aside so she could enter before him. He had nice manners. "Since you're the first one here, you get your choice of rooms. Keys are on the bureaus. Keep the door to guesthouse locked. Sometimes vagrants make their way back here and try to get in."

"First?" Then Skye remembered he'd said 'girls'.

"I have a couple of other female house guests scheduled to fly in for the party. I was so last minute pulling the party together no one could get a room. I even had to fly in an out-of-town caterer." He winked.

Skye hated winkers.

"When you've had a chance to freshen up, come on back to the main house and I'll show you the kitchen."

Tag watched Red follow Noah and felt a little sick. Of all the caterers in the country, how had Noah found and settled on Red? Skye's the Limit wasn't that well-known. There'd been an article about her in one of the more obscure sports journals after the Gems had won the World Series, but she wasn't exactly a household name. In a city famous for its food, she was a nobody.

A nobody who only had to look at him to make him hard.

A nobody he didn't want around while he debauched. Because Red wasn't the kind of woman who went in for debauchery. The last thing he wanted to do was hurt her. Yeah, he'd missed her while he was home, but a big part of his reason for coming to New Orleans was to forget about her.

The doorbell rang, startling him out of his funk. Since Noah was otherwise occupied, Tag opened the door. And nearly pissed himself.

"Tag! I didn't know you were visiting Noah." Terra Baldwin, his currently off-again woman friend breezed past him, pulling her utilitarian black suitcase. "It's nice to see you." She brushed her lips across his.

He resisted the urge to wipe away the caress. And hold his nose. He'd forgotten how much perfume she soaked in. "Terra. What a surprise." He purposely omitted *nice* or *pleasant*.

"Oh dear," she said. "You're still annoyed with me about not coming to your bedside when you were injured. I told you there were rumors of a revolution in Kabalastan. "

Still using her half-assed career as an excuse. Annoyed wasn't the word he'd use. The news was more important to her than their relationship. He'd known that on an intellectual level. "You overestimate my feelings. As usual." He purposely kept his tone cool. Disinterested.

She'd told him she'd been out of the country when he'd gotten hurt, but he'd heard a rumor she'd really been in Columbia—South Carolina, not South America. That not only had she been in town, but they had attended the same Halloween party. He'd been at Drake Dixon's place to keep an eye on Red because he'd heard bad stuff about Dixon and women, and allegedly Terra had been there wearing only a purple-feathered half-mask with silver beads. Her mouth had been available for whatever anyone wanted to stick in it.

Tag knew that was a double standard. He liked a blowjob as well as the next guy. And he and Terra had never talked about being exclusive. He was no saint. He liked fucking, and in different circumstances, he might have considered joining Dixon's Halloween orgy.

What irked him was Terra had been too busy to visit him, but not too busy to suck Dixon's cock. Hence the off-again, probably for good, relationship.

What troubled him more was wondering what other surprises Noah had in store.

"My leg is starting to bother me." Not a lie. "Noah's showing another guest where she'll be staying. He's putting the women in his guesthouse. They went that way." He jerked his head toward the back of the house.

His limp was a little more pronounced than necessary as he leaned on his cane and made his way back to Noah's den.

"I do hope you'll give me a chance to make amends," Terra called after him. "Maybe tonight."

He pretended not to hear her.

"Hi." Skye greeted the newcomer. The very familiar-looking new-comer. "Welcome to the girls' bunk. I'm Skye from Skye's the Limit catering. I guess we're housemates over the next few days. I'm in the violet room."

The dark-haired woman with eyes the color of fresh bruises gri-maced. "Noah is separating us by sex? How...quaint."

Skye recognized the woman now. She was a TV news reporter. Her name had been linked to Tag's in the past. Terra Baldwin. She worked for one of the minor cable news networks. Very minor. "Banished to the *garçonnière*."

"The what?"

"The house where single men lived on plantations before the Civil War." Skye had picked up a lot of information from the historical romance novels she'd read growing up. The oddest things stayed with her.

The other woman laughed. "I'm Terra Baldwin, by the way. Aren't you the caterer for the Gems?"

Skye couldn't help but be flattered. "Yes. The front office asked me if I'd work Mr. Nash's house party this week."

Terra shook her head. "Noah is a piece of work. Now Tag Gentry on the other hand... Do you know who else is here besides Tag?"

Skye tamped down the spurt of jealousy that flared. "I haven't seen anyone else. Mr. Nash said I was the first woman."

"Mr. Nash?" Terra laughed again.

The noise sounded forced to Skye.

"He's Noah. He won't want formality, even if you are working for him this week."

"It's a courtesy thing," Skye explained.

"Noah wouldn't know courtesy if it bit him in the ass."

Skye returned to the main house after she'd unpacked. Rather than disturb Mr. Nash, she went in search of the kitchen on her own. She found it almost immediately, as if she had culinary radar.

The facilities were okay. Less than ideal, but Skye could manage if she wasn't expected to produce anything too elaborate. She needed to get the details of the house party from Mr. Nash. How many guests? What meals would be required? Was there a household account to which she could charge purchases? What did he expect for the grand finale—Mardi Gras?

The situation still didn't feel right to her. Tag's former—maybe current—girlfriend was not someone she could be comfortable about. Tag had claimed he was no longer with Terra when he'd seduced Skye. Even so, she didn't like thinking that maybe she'd come between them.

"You'll be okay here?"

Skye jumped.

Noah Nash stood in the doorway. The man was quiet. Something about him—

"It's fine," she said. "As long as you don't want super fancy."

He shrugged. "It's Carnival. Everyone will be too wasted to appreciate anything elaborate."

"How many people are staying?"

"However many show up. I invited ten houseguests for the week. Maybe another fifty or so for Mardi Gras. And who knows who'll wander in off the streets. Things tend to get rowdy in the Quarter on Fat Tuesday."

Not very helpful. She tried again. "Do you want breakfast? Lunch? Supper? I forwarded my standard contract to you, but you only signed it. You didn't fill in any of the information I need."

"This is a house party. Emphasis on party. Do what you think is best."

Skye was starting to get annoyed. "Any requests?"

"I'll leave that up to you."

For someone who'd gone to the trouble of flying in his own caterer, Noah Nash didn't seem invested in his own event.

She need to research traditional Mardi Gras foods. She was trying to build her reputation as an events caterer, not just a sports caterer. Maybe if she kept telling herself Mardi Gras in New Orleans would look good on her résumé, she'd start to believe it.

Since the disaster of Drake Dixon's Halloween party, she'd been nervous. Some of her jobs were fine—the Board of Elections Election Night buffet, the Jaycee's Annual Harvest Ball, even Tubby Maldonado's Thanksgiving weekend wedding hadn't bothered her in the least. But private parties in people's homes? She turned down as many of those jobs as she could afford. Which wasn't many. Although she'd replaced her broken oven and range with used appliances, her state-of-the-art fantasy stove was still on her agenda. And at the rate she was going, forever out of reach.

If Nash hadn't played the Gems' card, she doubted she'd be in New Orleans.

"My main specialty is sports nutrition." She forced a smile. "I don't think that applies to Mardi Gras, Mr. Nash."

"Up to you," he repeated. "And please. Call me Noah."

"Buffet? Sit down? What kind of food do you want?"

"Your choice." He didn't seem at all interested. "I heard you're a great cook. I will leave everything in your competent hands. Oh and don't bother about tonight. We're going out."

Then he winked.

"You need to move me into the main house," Terra commanded.

Terra was not subtle. She was in full bitch mode too. Tag wondered what had set her off. Not that he cared. Or was even interested. Reacting to Terra was a habit, not an emotion.

Noah didn't seem to know what to do about her. "I don't have a room for you."

"This isn't church camp where you need to separate us by gender." She smiled at Tag. "If you don't have an extra room, I can bunk with Tag. It wouldn't be the first time."

"What's wrong with the guesthouse?" Noah asked.

"She can have my room," Tag said before Terra could answer. "Stairs are tough on my leg. I'll move to the guesthouse." Not a lie. Although he was managing fine with his cane, stairs were brutal. Besides, he didn't want to be in the same vicinity as Terra.

Red's presence had no bearing on his offer. None.

Noah's scowl deepened for a flash before his face smoothed. He became the genial buffoon of his reputation. "I didn't think about your injury and the stairs, Tag. "

Tag shrugged. He didn't want people thinking about his injury. He wanted to pretend he was whole. He wanted to forget the numbness down the side of his calf where the nerves were so badly damaged he probably would never regain feeling in that area. He wanted to forget the hours of brutal physical therapy Bluto the Torturer inflicted on him. He needed to believe he could fight his way back to home plate.

"It's no biggie." He refused to look at Terra. They owed each other nothing, not even good-byes.

"Well, if you're going to move to the guesthouse—" she began.

Tag cut her off. "We'll swap rooms. There's no point upsetting all Noah's preparations. Besides, I sleep better alone. I can't risk being accidently kicked."

"You just want a harem." Noah's joke didn't make Tag laugh.

Tag could smell Red in the purple bedroom. Even if he hadn't recognized her teal-colored overnight bag, he would have known she was the occupant by her scent alone. Her fragrance was far more delicate and natural than Terra's. Another bedroom opened off her bathroom. He dumped his bag in there. He knew Red. And she knew his boundaries.

He had let Noah carry his repacked suitcase down the stairs but had taken over from there. No point overplaying the gimp card.

Red wasn't around.

He took his time unpacking, hoping for a few more minutes of privacy.

Maybe Red had gone food shopping. She did that a lot. But more often than not in the morning, and it was now late afternoon. She was probably cooking supper for everyone. The reason she was there.

He was headed for the courtyard door when it swung open. A shaft of sunlight tangled in penny-colored curls.

"Hello."

Red stopped. Stared at him. "Did you need something?"

"I moved into the guesthouse. Terra wanted to be in the main house, and the stairs are tough on my leg, so we swapped. I'm in the blue bedroom. You and I are sharing a bathroom."

Her eyes widened when she realized what that meant. "Do you think that's such a good idea?"

Her voice was low. Sultry. As always, it did things to his spine. To his dick.

He stepped closer. "I think it's the perfect solution to a lot of issues." His cane clattered to the floor as he sauntered toward her. Pressed her against the wall. Let her know just how good of an idea it was as his mouth covered hers.

There was a brief moment of resistance, but Red melted as if she were an ice swan and he a volcano. Her lips parted. He cupped her ass and pulled her tight against his erection. She tried to get closer, but their clothes were in the way.

"God, I've missed you," he said when he was finally able to form coherent words. "Your room or mine?"

She pushed at his shoulders. "Not a good idea."

She was right. He'd come to New Orleans in part to forget about her.

So much for that plan.

"Why not?" He cupped her breast. He needed to suck on them. Needed to have her under him. His leg was up to fucking. He tugged at the back of her bra. Managed to unhook it.

"I'm not sure we should do this. Not here."

She was definitely right. He was in New Orleans to party.

Tomorrow. He'd start partying tomorrow.

He buried his face against her neck as he worked to rid her of more clothing. "Why not here? It's private. If I was a hundred percent, I'd pick you up and carry you to a bed, but you're going to have to walk."

"As if I've ever done anything else," she muttered.

"You run. You know it." If he didn't get inside her soon, he was going to come in his pants like some pubescent rookie. He released her. Grabbed her hand. Pulled her toward the purple bedroom.

She didn't resist. Thank God, she didn't resist. He closed the door. Red was naked by the time he reached the bed. No subterfuge. No false modesty. But she wasn't a ball-breaker either. Not like the women who waited outside the stadium doors or in the hotel lobbies looking for happy-ever-after in a quickie.

Red was beautiful. She didn't wear makeup, as far as he could tell, so there was never black gunk under her eyes. Her copper-bright curls spread out on the pillow. He knew she didn't fuss with it, only to pull it back when she was in chef mode. She never complained about having small tits or a big ass or any number of other flaws women had wanted reassurance about over the years. Which made her perfect. She didn't wax or shave her pussy, either, which was a nice change for him. He felt like he was with a woman instead of a little girl.

He knelt at her feet and spread her legs. His leg had been in a cast most of the time they'd been together, so she'd had to do most of the giving, and by God it was her turn to do a little taking. He swiped a finger down her slit to check her readiness. She was wet. Slick. And he'd left the damned condoms in his room.

"Don't move," he said. His throat felt tight, as if being with Red again was strangling him. "I'll be right back."

"Are there condoms in your shaving kit? I'll get them." Red took her time climbing off the bed. Strolling to the bathroom as lazy as a Sunday afternoon. Fetching a strip of gold-wrapped condoms.

"Planning on being busy this vacation?" she asked as she locked the door to the bathroom.

He didn't bother trying to identify the catch in her voice. "Never know when I'm going to need them."

Her smile was slow. She tossed the condoms on the bed and stood in front of him. "Looks like you're wearing too many clothes." She unbuttoned his shirt, turning the chore into foreplay.

Her fingers brushed his bare flesh Tweaked his nipples, which sent most of his blood rushing to his dick. By the time she slipped her palms into the waistband of his slacks, he knew if he wasn't foaming at the mouth, he ought to be. He reached for his belt buckle, but she stopped him.

"Let me. I never got to open many presents when I was a kid. My dad wasn't big on holidays."

He was dizzy. Good thing the bed was only a step away.

The buckle gave way. She was careful with his zipper, which was about ready to separate on its own. Again, a few teasing touches against the cotton of his boxers nearly sent him to the ceiling.

"I hope you're enjoying this," he said. "Because in about thirty seconds you're going on your back and getting fucked the way I've always wanted to fuck you."

"Promises, promises," she murmured, then yanked his pants to his ankles.

He pulled her onto the bed with him. Grabbed the condoms. Managed to open one and get it on. He didn't need to spread her thighs, because she was ready for him. Inviting him in.

Then he was balls-deep inside her. He lost all awareness except of her. How she felt around him. How the walls of her pussy clung to his cock, creating a friction so incredible he knew he wouldn't last. Red met him thrust for thrust. Her soft cries spurred him on, whimpers turning to moans as her climax seized her. Her arms tightened around his ribs. Thighs clamped his waist. Deep clenching massaged his cock when he thrust. Red might have moved slowly to tease him, but she always came pretty quickly. She didn't need hours of foreplay to be ready for him.

Strangely enough, her orgasm subdued his need to come right away. He didn't mind. Being inside her was the only place he could think to be.

He slowed his pace. She unlocked her ankles from the small of his back and dragged her tongue down the side of his neck, igniting deep tremors in him. He couldn't have stopped his climax even if he'd wanted to.

He braced his weight on his arms as he waited for his breath to even out. His leg ached, but he wouldn't give in to the pain.

"These sleeping arrangements suit me much better than what Noah had in mind," he said.

"What sleeping arrangements? I didn't get any sleep."

He laughed. Red always made him laugh.

He rolled off her, and she sat up. Her eyes widened as she took in the mess that had once been his leg.

He wanted to hide. Cringe in shame. Yeah, they'd had sex since he'd been out of the cast, but always late at night. Always in dim light or in the dark. So this was her first real look at what that punk asshole from New York had done to him with his cleats. Surgical scars. The place where his shinbone had burst through his skin. Red, angry welts. Frankenstein leg.

She extended one finger toward the largest scar. He flinched when the warmth of her flesh breathed against his. An aura of healing. "Do they hurt?

He shook his head. "Not the skin. But inside. Yeah. It hurts." Sometimes it hurt so badly he wanted to cry. Sometimes Bluto the Torturer, his physical therapist, pushed him so far he couldn't swallow his screams. But if he wanted to resurrect his career, he needed to work. And work meant pain.

She leaned forward and brushed her mouth across the worst of the scar tissue. Lapped her tongue against him.

He flinched. But he didn't stop her. He didn't think he *could* stop her. She gently laved each stitch mark. Too bad her kisses couldn't heal his wounds.

The gentle ministrations had another effect on him. His cock twitched. Hardened. Strained toward her.

Another condom. Red on her back again. Welcoming him in without judgment or disgust. Even he was disgusted at the way his flesh had betrayed him under the pressure of another player's cleats.

Slow. He went slowly this time. Kissing every inch of her skin. Returning the gift of acceptance she had given him.

SKYE BLINKED BACK the tears trying to clog her eyes. Tag had been hurt trying to be good to his team. She'd had no idea how badly his leg had been messed up. Seeing the evidence shocked her. No wonder he was bitter. She'd seen hints of his anger during the World Series, and now some of his surliness was understandable.

She wanted to kiss away not only his physical scars but whatever troubled him.

And she shouldn't feel that way. Their relationship was headed nowhere but Hurtsville for her and a sometimes memory for him. She hoped he would remember her with fondness.

In the aftermath, lying in Tag's arms and wishing the outside world would go away, it intruded in the worst possible way.

At least she'd locked the door between the bathroom and her room.

"What is it?" Skye tried to speak as if she'd just wakened instead of climaxing.

"Have you seen Tag?" The voice sounded like Terra.

Tag's gaze locked with Skye's. He shook his head.

"Why would I know where Tag is?"

"No one has seen him in a while, and we're getting ready to go out."

"Sorry. I can't help you." Skye replied.

She held her breath until she heard someone banging around in Tag's room. That was all it took. She was pissed. She motioned for Tag to stay put, then pulled on her robe. She unlocked the door and stormed through the bathroom.

Terra was going through the bureau drawers.

"What do you think you're doing? Investigating his disappearance?" Skye asked. "Do you think he's hiding in his dresser?"

Terra slammed the drawer and whirled around. She didn't even have the grace to look guilty. "What are you doing in Tag's room?"

"How do you know this is Tag's room?" Skye asked.

"I recognize his bag."

"I was under the impression you'd moved out of the guesthouse. You have no business in any room here."

"Since when are you the concierge?" Terra's sneer ruined the effect of her perfectly made-up face. Too bad an expression couldn't neutralize her heavy perfume.

"I'll let Tag know you were going through his stuff." Skye turned to leave.

"Wait."

The hair on Skye's nape prickled, but she didn't turn to face Terra.

"How do you know Tag?" Terra asked.

"I cater the Columbia Gems' home games."

"Right. We talked about that earlier. Didn't you cater Drake Dixon's Halloween party?"

Forget nape hairs prickling. Skye's stood on end and started doing the Wave. "I did."

"And you were hired to cater this Mardi Gras party?"

"That's why I'm here. Does it matter?"

Terra abruptly changed the topic. "If you see Tag, let him know I'm looking for him, will you? "

She sounded friendly. As if she and Skye were buddies. Pals. Going to meet for wine and girl talk next week.

"If I see him."

Skye waited until she heard the door close behind Terra before she returned to her room.

"Well played," Tag said as he reached for her.

"I'm locking the front door," Skye replied. She let Tag pull her into bed. "Mr. Nash said he sometimes has a vagrant problem. And we need to lock our room doors too."

"I wonder who else he plans putting out here."

"There are two other bedrooms." The guesthouse was bigger than her entire third-floor apartment back in Columbia.

"I got the impression he'd planned to segregate everyone by sex," Tag said. "I told him I didn't mind sleeping with the ladies. I didn't mention you were the main attraction."

"It's backward," she said. "On Creole plantations, the bachelors were in the separate house and the women were in the main house."

Tag quirked an eyebrow. "And how would you know that?"

"I read a lot of romance novels when I was growing up." What else was she supposed to do when she'd never lived in a town long enough to make friends, and her father belittled her efforts to make them a home? "This building, if it were on a plantation, would be called the garçonnière. The wild bachelors and other unmarried men would live here. The older folks needed to keep a closer eye on the virtue of the young women."

"Fascinating." He circled one of her nipples with his forefinger. "I'll bet you are really good in trivia tournaments."

Her nipple puckered, but she wasn't in the mood for more sex. Not since Terra had nearly interrupted them. "I need to lock the front door."

"Noah has a key. And won't he think it's funny when he can't bring his other guests back here?"

"Terra was searching your belongings."

"What?" He pinched the tip of her nipple.

"I caught Terra rummaging through your stuff. You could always say someone had been in your room, without mentioning names, and that you were worried about a thief."

Tag released her. Sat up. "Why would Terra be going through my things?"

"Sniffing your underwear?" Skye meant it as a joke.

Tag scowled. "You sound jealous."

"Why should I be jealous? You and I are friends. Right? Only friends?"

She was jealous, and she hated that the little crush she'd developed on him during the baseball season had morphed into an uncontrollable monster. She didn't merely want him—she *craved* Tag Gentry. Developing a self-destructive streak this late in life wasn't very bright.

She rolled off the bed. "I need to take a shower."

She pushed on Tag's chest when it looked like he was going to follow her. "You need to take your own shower. Alone." She was his secret. It was probably better for both of them if they kept it that way.

TAG STUDIED HIS room while Red showered. Traces of Terra's perfume lingered in the air, but all that meant was she'd been in the vicinity. He opened the top bureau drawer, where he'd unpacked his boxers and T-shirts. Yeah, someone had moved things around. He was a neat packer, the habit of a man who lived more than half his life on the road.

Terra traveled too, so one would think she'd developed the same tendency. For a reporter, she was awfully sloppy when it came to snooping. Unless Red had interrupted before Terra could clean up after herself.

But why would she search his belongings?

He wasn't a story. The only time Tag had ever seen her truly invest herself in something was when she was hot on the trail of something she thought might be a juicy news piece. She didn't even get that involved in sex. At least, not with him.

Tag sat on the end of his bed. He wasn't a story, but his career was. Especially if he could never reclaim it. The team had been circumspect about the extent of his injuries. The HIPAA laws worked in his favor. He knew there was a lot of speculation about his future. The stories about him not reporting to spring training with the other pitchers and catchers had claimed more airtime than the truth warranted. Because of the timing of his injury. The why of his injury. Any other player on any other team would not be in the national news as often. But because he'd been injured making the out that sent his team to the World Series for the first time, and because the Gems had won without him, he was still national news.

Terra loved the offbeat story.

Terra had an inside track to him.

But why would she think he had any of his medical records on him when visiting New Orleans?

Because he would be seeing a physical therapist to keep up his rehab routine, and licensing requirements varied from state to state. Plus Hector Michaud, the therapist Bluto the Torturer had found for Tag, was a specialist who had developed a radical new form of therapy that might be the answer to Tag's inability to recuperate quickly.

He limped to the armoire where he'd stowed his bag. Hopefully Red had interrupted Terra before she'd gotten that far. Why would she think he'd keep important papers in his underwear drawer?

He'd put the documents in the zipper lining of the suitcase lid. They appeared untouched.

Red was right about keeping the door to the guesthouse locked. And locking their rooms.

Bluto the Torturer probably should have faxed the reports to Hector Michaud. Or even better, Tag should have brought Bluto with him to New Orleans. Except Bluto wasn't a licensed physical therapist in Louisiana and didn't have the facility or equipment to do what needed to be done. The problem was Tag didn't trust faxes or e-mails with his information. The electronic highway was too vulnerable to hijackers, so he carried his paperwork with him.

In fact, he had an appointment at nine o'clock that night. The late hour was the only time Michaud could fit him in. He glanced at his watch. Being with Red made him lose track of time. He couldn't afford to miss even one minute of therapy. Not if he wanted his career back.

Noah Nash and his guests were the kind of people who stayed up all night and never ate breakfast. Skye had gone to bed early, sleeping deeply in sheets that smelled of Tag. Scented by sex with Tag. And she hadn't wakened except when Tag returned from the dinner she hadn't been invited to and slipped under the covers with her and curled around her back.

She arose with the sun, kissed a still-sleeping Tag on the cheek, and called her cab driver from the previous day. He'd given her his card when she'd asked him to wait until she knew what she was getting into. Kahil had assured her he knew where to take her to look at fresh produce so she could get a sense of what was available. Not the French Market, which was too commercial for her needs, but a farmers' market. Every city had a place where chefs, greengrocers, and other food people could pick out what they wanted. Until she knew what was available, she couldn't plan the menu for Noah's party.

She prepared a pot of coffee and a platter of beignets and left them in the dining room of the main house before she left.

Kahil drove her around, pointing out several parade routes. "Nothing until after five tonight," he explained.

Maybe parades didn't clog the street, but the throngs of people did a fine job all by themselves. Working at the baseball stadium had numbed her to crowds to a certain extent, but this? She could never become inured to this madness.

The French Market turned out to be nicer than she'd thought, but the Crescent City Farmers Market stole her heart. She wandered for a couple of hours, took in a cooking demonstration, and basked in the aromas of freshly dug root vegetables, flowers, and faintly briny shrimp.

"It's located in a different place with different vendors every day of the week," Kahil explained.

When she finally returned to Noah's house, Tag was nowhere to be found.

"Get over yourself," she muttered. Working with food usually vanquished her troubles. Terra Baldwin wasn't even a trouble. A blip. Skye wasn't going be jealous. She and Tag had established their boundaries when they'd first started having sex. Friends. With fabulous benefits. Nothing more.

She barricaded herself in her room and resumed her Internet research on traditional Mardi Gras cuisine. She learned the colors of Mardi Gras were green for faith, gold for power, and purple for justice. She could work with that. Green and purple cabbage slaw with bits of pineapple. A salad with purple, green, and yellow bell peppers. Definitely a buffet. A simple spread for a bunch of people who were only going to get drunk wasn't such a big deal. Still, she did have her reputation to uphold. Healthier eating had to be part of the plan.

Skye lay down for a nap midafternoon. She hadn't gotten much sleep the previous evening. She hadn't known a man could perform so many times in one night without the aid of medications, but Tag had educated her.

The shower running in the adjacent bathroom roused her only for a moment. A little while later, another commotion in the hall disturbed her, but she managed to fall back asleep. She woke again at five, still alone. And that was okay. She'd never learned the art of small talk. How to be social. She'd rather read than attend a cocktail party. Unless she was catering. She didn't need to mingle to feed people.

Her phone had a good selection of e-books on it. It had been a godsend in Florida, where she didn't have her building rehab or other jobs to occupy her time when she wasn't feeding the team. So she curled up on the yellow-and-lavender striped window seat and prepared to get lost in the past.

She didn't hear the discreet rapping on her bathroom door at first. She slid off the window cushion and went to the door. "Who is it?"

"Tag."

She unlocked the door and let him in.

"You were expecting someone else through the bathroom?"

"I wouldn't put anything past Terra Baldwin."

"Smart of you." Tag closed the door and relocked it.

He didn't look well. His skin was pale. Deep lines bracketed his eyes and mouth. "I need a favor from you."

"That's what friends are for," she quipped.

He grimaced.

That was when she noticed he carried a manila clasp envelope.

"I think you're right about Terra searching in my room."

"I caught her," Skye reminded him. "What's in the envelope?"

"Bluto's report. For the physical therapist he fixed me up with while I'm down here. I think it's what Terra is looking for. Everyone knows about the broken shinbone, but the other stuff—well, it's not public. I'd like you to hold on to the report for me."

"Why didn't Bluto just fax or e-mail the records?"

"I don't trust either method. It's a lot more secure if I carry them myself. So will you hold on to them for me?"

"Why?"

"So Terra won't find them."

"Why would Terra want your medical— Oh."

"Yeah." He extended the envelope.

Skye took it from him. "Of course." She went to her bureau and opened the top drawer, then swished around her undies until the envelope was covered by pastel fabric.

Then she turned to Tag. "Are you okay? You look a little—"

"Beat?" Tag offered. "I am. I had a physical therapy session a couple of hours ago, and this Hector Michaud guy makes Bluto look like one of those stupid Internet kittens."

Skye knew Bluto. If Tag compared him to a blue-eyed ball of fluff, the New Orleans PT practitioner had to be a sadist.

"Are you going out to supper with the rest of the guests?" Skye asked. He really didn't look well.

"I have to. Do you want to come with me?"

Skye shook her head. "I'll be fine. I'm good at entertaining myself."

"Don't entertain yourself too thoroughly." Tag leered, and her female bits clenched. "I plan to leave as soon as the main course is over. People don't realize PT is more exhausting than playing every day. Then you and I can entertain each other. Leave your bathroom door unlocked."

Her head suggested she tell him no, but was overruled by every other part of her body. "See you later then."

Tag thought dinner would never end. The food wasn't nearly as good as Red's. Nor was the company. Terra wasn't subtle. She'd latched on to him as soon as he'd arrived—alone in his own car—at the restaurant. Rather than make a scene, he'd accepted her sitting next to him. That didn't mean he was going to engage in small talk with her. She had nothing to say he wanted to hear.

He spent most of the meal wondering why he'd ever bothered with her. Maybe some half-baked idea that she could help him land a broadcasting job after he'd retired. But he didn't want to be stuck in a broadcast booth explaining baseball games to anyone, especially if it meant he had to keep Terra in his life.

She tried to leave with him, and he had to resort to rudeness. He'd never been rude to a woman in his life, but Terra ignored all his subtle disinclinations.

"I have things to do, and you're not welcome." He tried to keep his voice low, but the way its natural timbre carried was one of the reasons Terra insisted he'd be a great broadcaster.

Conversation around the table stopped. Terra's cheeks brightened. He hadn't meant to embarrass her, but frustration with her made him careless about modulating his voice.

Some days it seemed like the only person not pushing him to do or be something or someone else was Red.

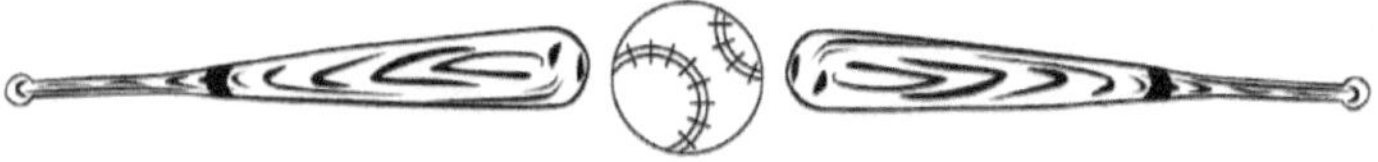

Skye was sitting in the window seat when a shadow slithered through the courtyard. Her room was dark because all she needed was the light from her phone to read her book. She'd thought about staging a seduction or at least setting a romantic scene for Tag, but she wasn't the romantic type. There were already fresh flowers in her bedroom, courtesy of Mr. Nash. Even if she managed to find a bunch of candles in the main house, she couldn't be certain when Tag would be returning. And she'd feel ridiculous. So she wore her usual fleece running shorts and oversize sleep shirt to read. The only way the night could be better would be if she were home, in her own bed.

The sounds of the city were muted in the back of the courtyard. The narrow streets of the French Quarter were alive with tourists celebrating. Kahil the Cabbie had told her about the krewes, the organizations that sponsored floats in the big parade and usually held their own smaller events throughout the city in the weeks leading up to Mardi Gras. New Orleans was not a restful city.

Even so, she heard the scratch of the key in the lock of the guesthouse door. The creaks of door hinges and old floorboards under someone's weight.

Five minutes later, the door to the shared bathroom opened, and Tag stepped into her room. "Why are you sitting in the dark?"

"I was using my e-reader app. It's easier to read in the dark." Skye slipped off the window seat and crossed to the bedside table, where she turned on the lamp. The low wattage bulb created a shallow puddle of tallow-colored light. "Better?"

Tag didn't look any better than he had before he'd gone to dinner. He wore only boxers of an indeterminate color. Dark hair peppered his pecs and abs. She glanced at his leg. At the ugly legacy of a rookie trying to make an impression.

Lust slammed low into her belly. She crossed the room. Reached for his hands. His huge, calloused hands. Even the off months since his injury hadn't been able to soften what years of catching baseballs had done to his palms.

Skye led him to her bed. He freed his hands from hers and gripped the shoulder seams of her sleep shirt. Tugged. She raised her arms, and he pulled the garment over her head. She slipped her fingers into the waistband of his boxers and yanked them down, while he returned the favor with her track shorts. They stepped out of their clothes together.

"I didn't stay for dessert," Tag said and tipped her toward the mattress.

Skye landed on her back. She started to scoot closer to the headboard, but Tag grabbed her ankles.

"No. Right here. Just like this." He knelt at the foot of the bed. Parted her thighs.

Skye's breath hitched. Her stomach muscles quivered as Tag's warm breath stirred her pubic hair. "Tag."

"Hush." Then his tongue touched her. His huge hands spanned her inner thighs, holding her open for his pleasure. Her pleasure. A few hesitant licks had Skye reaching for the ceiling. The headboard. Anything to anchor her. She settled for wadding the comforter in her fists. Just in time.

Tag delved. His entire mouth closed over her. Labia. Clit. Opening to her vagina. He sucked. He licked. He nibbled. His hands slid from her thighs to her bottom, where he palmed her ass cheeks. Squeezed them. Used them to lift her closer to his mouth.

Skye released the bedspread and reached for Tag's silky dark hair. The soles of her feet, flat against the mattress, were hot, as if someone were applying fire to them. The heat flickered up her ankles. Up her calves. Through her knees. Licked at her thighs.

"Well, isn't this interesting?"

The strange voice barely registered with Skye. Tag lifted his head. Stopped his magic mouth. Skye released his hair.

"What are you doing here?" Tag's voice was husky.

Skye turned to face the intruder.

Terra. In a filmy nightgown. Gripping a gold-foil-capped bottle. Droplets of condensation trickled from the dark green glass to the rug.

"I was coming to you to see if we couldn't mend our fences." Terra shrugged. "Do you mind if I join you?"

Skye jackknifed upright. Reached for a cover, but Tag pinned her to the mattress, and the comforter wouldn't budge beneath her weight. "Yes, I mind." Skye's voice was barely a squeak. "How did you get in here?"

"I knocked on Tag's door. When there was no answer, I came in. Followed the sounds through the bathroom."

"I mean into the guesthouse." Skye could swear she'd heard Tag lock the door after he came in.

"I moved back this afternoon. The main house isn't as comfortable as here."

"You mean Tag is staying here."

Terra lifted her chin. "Your interpretation."

Tag climbed onto the mattress. He sat between the women, shielding Skye's nudity from Terra. "You heard Red. She doesn't want you in her room."

Terra's gaze shifted from Skye to Tag. If eyes could touch, every inch of Tag's body would have been caressed—or molested. A horrible invasion of privacy.

"I don't mind sharing," Terra said. She licked her lips.

"But I do." Skye thought her heart might leap out of her chest and into her throat.

"Red has spoken," Tag said. "Now, are you going to leave of your own accord or do I have to escort you from the room? Let me assure you. You will not like the second thing. Ten seconds."

"You've changed," Terra said.

"My priorities aren't yours. Eight."

Terra turned.

"Leave through this bedroom door. I want to see you gone." His tone was hard. Unforgiving. "Six."

Terra flinched, then walked into the hall.

Tag leaped from the bed and closed the door. "Damn it. I keep forgetting to lock the hall door." While he stalked into the bathroom, Skye wrapped herself in the comforter. She was shaking by the time Tag returned.

"I locked the door to my room," he said as he twisted the lock on Skye's bathroom door. "I didn't know she'd moved back."

"I might have heard her this afternoon, but I was napping, and when something woke me up, I was really muzzy and fell back to sleep."

"It's not your fault." Tag stood at the foot of the bed.

"Did you do a lot of...sharing with her? I mean, I know you two are together. Everyone in Columbia knows it."

"Were together. We split the sheets several months ago."

"You didn't answer my question." Skye couldn't shake the memory of what she'd seen at Drake Dixon's Halloween party from her mind.

Twosomes, threesomes, even as many as five people, naked people, reenacting the *Kama Sutra*. Together. Definitely out of her league.

"Terra is bold. I'm not shy." He sat on the edge of the mattress. "Does that bother you?"

Skye shook her head. If she couldn't ask Tag about such things, who else could she ask? "I'm curious."

"What do you want to know?"

Keep it light, she reminded herself. "Nothing. I don't need the details of your past. We're just friends. Remember?"

"And friends talk to each other," Tag said. "What do you want to know?"

Skye hesitated before blurting out her question. "Have you ever been in a threesome?"

He stared at her for a long moment before he nodded. "A lot of rookie baseball players have opportunities to explore things outside of their normal. Some guys buy fast cars. Some guys get into doping. There are women who will do anything to sleep with a professional ball player."

"I'm not asking about a lot of anonymous rookie players." Her face was so hot she thought her cheeks might burst into flames.

Tag sighed. "Okay. Here's the deal. You know I grew up on a farm with a shitload of siblings."

Skye nodded. "I read that in your bio."

"There was this girl. Christi Fellows. Her father was the head deacon of the local Baptist church. Christi had a crush on my older brother. And my younger brother. And me. And eventually we all...took advantage of opportunities." He smiled, as if he were enjoying the memory, his eyes half-closed.

"You shared her."

"She shared herself with us. Hell, it was her idea. I don't think it would have occurred to any of us guys that more than one of us could fuck her at a time."

Skye was fascinated in spite of herself. Things inside her body contracted, expanded. The thought of another woman didn't interest her. But—

"Do you want the dirty details?" Tag's silvery eyes gleamed through his eyelashes.

"If you don't mind sharing those." She couldn't believe she'd said that. But she wanted to know.

Tag slid closer to her. Slipped his hand under the comforter until he found her breast. "One of us would suck her left tit." He lowered his head until he could pull her nipple into his mouth. As he sucked, he pressed a palm against her breastbone.

Skye collapsed onto the pillows.

He released her nipple. "Another one of us would suck her right tit." Again, he followed the words with action, while he tweaked her left nipple with his fingers. The scruff of his beard abraded her skin, but she didn't mind.

After a moment he stopped. "And I already showed you what the third brother would suck. Imagine if you can, because I can't, what it would be like to have two men sucking your boobs, and a third going at your pussy."

He was right. Her imagination wasn't up to it.

"We'd do that, changing positions every so often, until she would come. And Christi always came. Loud and long. Next it was our turn."

Skye's breathing was heavier. Her breasts felt fuller. Her labia, engorged. "You mean like this?" She scooted down until she could take Tag's penis into her mouth.

"Exactly like that." His exhalations matched hers.

Skye worked her tongue around the underside of his cock, then swallowed it as deeply as she could. Which wasn't very far. Tag's build was generous.

His fingers tangled in her hair as he controlled the pace of her action. He smelled faintly salty, like stale sea air. His penis twitched.

"Okay, that's good," he said. "We don't want to rush things, and you have this habit of getting me too excited."

She raised her head, dragging her tongue along the length of him as she slowly worked to release him.

He reached for a condom. Rolled it on, then lay on the bed. "Remember when my leg was in a cast. When we first started fucking?"

Skye nodded.

"Well, Christi would ride one of us just like that at the same time she was sucking another brother off." His cock was completely upright and waiting for her.

Skye swung her leg over his body. She had this part down pat. He'd been in a leg cast for weeks. She'd never had as much sex as she'd had during that time period. Taking her time now, she lowered herself onto his cock, wanting the moment to last as long as she could stretch it.

His eyelids drifted shut as his lips parted. A soft moan escaped. "I love fucking you," he whispered. He grasped her bottom in his oversized palms.

"Wait a minute," she whispered back. "I thought I was fucking you."

He smiled. For a moment, she wished she had her phone nearby so she could snap a photo of him looking exactly like that. Exactly like that was how she wanted to remember him for the rest of her life.

"Okay," he said a moment later. "Christi was sucking off one of us, riding another one of us. Guess what the third brother was doing?"

"Playing with her breasts?"

"Wrong answer."

Tag moved one hand from her butt cheek to her butt crack.

An unfamiliar clenching threw Skye off her rhythm.

One of his fingers brushed her anus. She felt the instant pucker. And dizzy. So very, very dizzy.

He pressed against the opening.

"Oh." Her involuntary response didn't stop him. He worked the tip of a finger inside. Her muscles contracted around the intrusion.

"Christi really loved getting fucked in the ass. Especially if there was another cock in her pussy or someone was chowing down on her clit."

Skye didn't know what to think. What to feel. Emotionally feel. She was well aware of the physical sensations swirling in her body.

"We didn't always fuck her at the same time. There are as many variations on that theme as there are pitches in baseball. Sometimes I'd go down on her while Hunter was in her ass. Cooper liked to titty fuck her, mostly because he didn't have to wear a condom to do it. He'd lick her tits all over, mostly on the inside, until her skin was nice and slick. And she had big ones too. She'd press them together with her upper arms while Cooper sat on her rib cage and slid his cock between her tits and into her mouth."

Tag burrowed deeper. Moved his finger in a circular pattern, which made Skye gasp.

"Lean forward," he instructed.

She did, and he pulled her left nipple into his mouth. Sucked hard. Nipped ever so slightly. She kept moving on his cock, but her rhythm turned erratic. His finger kept probing. Stroking. Invading.

Orgasm sneaked up on her, taking over her body and stealing her mind. Tag held her as she shuddered. Kissed her between her gasps for breath. Held her on the mattress when she might have soared into the ether and never returned. And when her brain finally started functioning again, when her essence rediscovered her skin and crawled back inside, she realized Tag hadn't come. His cock was still thick and hard inside her.

He tipped her to her side, never losing the connection. "Look at me, Red."

Skye opened her eyes.

"Did you like that?"

She nodded. Just once.

"Would you like me to put my cock in your ass and fuck you that way? I've heard it hurts the first time, and we don't have any lube. The last thing in the world I want to do is hurt you."

Too late.

"I'm really close to coming, but I want it to be your decision." His normally gray eyes were a wash of darkness in his face as he looked at her. Really studied her.

Her thoughts were a jumble of contradictions. She didn't fear possible pain. Regrets? That was another story. She didn't want any regrets when it came to Tag. But she loved him. She couldn't deny it, not to herself, not any longer.

"Is that what you want?" she whispered.

He stroked a stray curl off her forehead. "I want whatever you want." He pressed as deeply into her vagina as he could. Held himself there.

Skye detected the faintest of tremors in his arms. "What do I need to do?"

Tag closed his eyes. Tightly. As if offering up a prayer.

"I've done it in two positions. The first is with you on your back, your legs up, just like when we fuck missionary, but instead of being in your pussy, I'll stick my cock in your ass. The other is doggie-style, with you on your hands and knees and me behind you."

"How's your leg feeling?"

Tag kissed the tip of her nose. "If it starts to bother me, on your back you'll go."

He slowly withdrew from her and helped her get to her hands and knees. "Lean forward a bit, so your ass is in the air."

She complied, feeling foolish. Involuntarily jerked when he dipped his fingers into her vagina, then circled his target to spread the slickness from her orgasm and ease his way. And repeated the gesture. Flinched as a finger nudged harder. Deeper.

"Don't tense up. It will only make it worse," he said as he worked a second finger inside her. His breath was hot against her neck. "You're really tight, and I don't want to hurt you."

Too late. The realization wouldn't go away. The acknowledgment changed nothing.

Skye rested her head on her folded arms and tried to control her body's natural instinct to expel his fingers. Her heart's natural instinct screamed at her to flee this intimacy that would lead nowhere.

"I think you're ready for me." His voice was more of a vibration of his chest against her back than a sound.

Stretching. Subtle. Gradual. She kept her breathing slow and steady.

"Are you okay?" Tag asked.

"Yes."

It hurt. Only a little.

"Do you want me to stop?"

She shook her head.

She had no idea how long it took for Tag to rock his way fully inside her. But eventually he was there, by inserting a little, with drawing a little, inserting a little more.

"Dear Sweet Jesus," he said.

Something dripped onto Skye's back. Drool? Perspiration?

"No, I'm Skye."

"Yes, you are."

He began to thrust. Slowly and gently at first, but as she became more accommodating, he picked up his pace. The sensations were so completely different from vaginal or oral sex Skye wasn't sure she'd be able to climax. Not that it mattered. Tag had already taken care of her. This was for him.

"Can you reach your clit?" he whispered against her ear. His chest hair lightly abraded the skin of her back.

"Maybe." But she didn't want to move. Didn't want to upset her precarious balance between the uncertainty she was doing the right thing by being with him and indifference to the heartbreak loving him would bring. She decided she could indulge a little while longer. Ignore the inevitable outcome. Twenty-eight years of being responsible hadn't earned her a thing. Maybe this extended fling with Tag was her reward for too many years of playing life safe.

"It'll be better for you if you play with yourself."

He lifted himself from her back. Grasped her hips with both hands.

She dislodged her left hand and tried to touch herself between the legs, but the position was too awkward.

No wonder his friend Christi had liked oral and anal sex at the same time. Maybe Skye should have chosen missionary position.

A moment later, Tag increased his pace. In a few strokes, he shuddered. Held himself balls-deep inside her ass. She could feel every twitch of his cock, every jerk as he ejaculated into his condom. Then he collapsed. On top of her. Still inside her. And she got to experience his shrinkage as the blood left his penis for other parts of his body.

It took a while for him to be able to roll away and deal with the condom. Too much time. She struggled with her rampaging emotions.

His limp seemed more pronounced when he made his way to the bathroom. She half expected him to return to his own room, but he didn't.

They snuggled together under the covers.

"Did I satisfy your curiosity?" His voice was a low rumble against her ear.

"Mostly."

"Only mostly?" He laughed. "What else is there to know?"

"Well, when Terra came in, there was you, me, and her. Two women, one man. Not that I'm interested in sex with another woman."

"Yeah. You like cock. My cock."

She loved his cock, but that was her secret.

"Have you ever done it with two women?"

"Yeah. I've tried it. But you know what? I like being able to concentrate on one woman. Making sure one woman is satisfied. Trying to pleasure two women divides my attention too much."

"Oh what a politically correct answer." She smiled against his chest. Quickly lapped at his skin. He tasted wonderful.

He was wonderful.

"It's the truth," he insisted. But he followed it with a laugh.

She snuggled closer, wishing this was reality, not an interlude. "So whatever happened to Christi the deacon's daughter?"

Tag choked. Then he said, "You have to promise not to laugh."

"I swear."

"Well, according to my younger brother, she got pregnant. Claimed a neighbor's border collie raped her. Her father shot the dog."

"That's not funny."

"I know. Poor dog."

Skye punched his arm.

"I swear to God, that's what Cooper told me." He pulled her even closer. "Red?"

She didn't answer.

"Hey. Are you asleep already?"

"Nope."

"Then why didn't you answer? Because my brother told me a bad joke?"

"Because my name is Skye. Everyone calls me that." She didn't think she'd ever heard him say her name. When he wasn't calling her Red, he called her by her given name: Celeste. Which wasn't such a bad name when he said it.

"Not me. I'm not everyone, and you should know that. And there's something else you should already know, but I'm going to say it anyway. I realize we're just friends and all, but what we just did? Everything we just did? You should be careful about doing it again. With another person. Not everyone is as a good of a friend as I am."

Friday, February 24 — Krewe of the Bosom Buddies Parade

Skye carried in bags of fresh produce to Noah Nash's kitchen. Kahil had told her about a place specializing in natural foods with an emphasis on Mardi Gras-colored ones. Unfortunately, he couldn't drive her that day, because it was the Muslim Sabbath. She discovered the purple palette didn't stop at eggplants, beets, and cabbage. Skye went crazy on bell peppers, kale, fingerling potatoes, asparagus, and violets. There was no reason the holiday debauchery had to include unhealthy eating.

She'd barely made it back before the Krewe of the Bosom Buddies Parade started. The streets of Quarter had been filled with people waiting for the parade to begin.

If things were happening as usual, Noah and most of his guests would still be in bed, sleeping off the previous evening's entertainment.

The married couple who functioned as a chauffeur, gardener, and housekeeper was in the kitchen. Turned out Selena was also the cook. Skye apologized for usurping the woman's kitchen, but it was still an awkward moment.

"I don't know why the boss hired an outsider to cook for his party," Selena told Skye. "My family has worked for the family for generations. Our cooking has always been more than satisfactory."

"I don't get it either," Skye said. "I'd love your help with the party. I know nothing about Mardi Gras."

"Joe and I have the night off for a change. You're on your own."

"What kind of parties does Mr. Nash usually throw?" Skye knew nothing about Mardi Gras, knew nothing about New Orleans, or Noah Nash. She figured the only reason she'd been hired was as a favor to Tag.

"Mr. Nash? He's a perpetual guest." Selena's dark gaze slid past Skye's shoulder. She shrugged. "Whatever. Joe and I are looking forward to our holiday."

"Oh. I thought with the guesthouse and all, Mr. Nash had regular house parties."

"Didn't I just tell you he's the perpetual guest?"

"Then who—"

Selena snorted. "If you don't know who you're working for, maybe you'd better find another line of business."

"Noah Nash hired me." Skye had his name on a contract. His signature.

"Good for you." Selena grinned at Skye. "I have to start on the bathrooms."

Tag didn't remember Noah being a party animal. There were players who were, but Noah had never hung with them. Maybe retirement and its subsequent boredom had turned him into the man Tag now saw and didn't like.

This house party was turning out not to be much fun. For starters, if he went out with the gang at night, he would never make it to his morning physical therapy session. Each morning, as he walked through the center hall of the main house, the place was so quiet, so completely lifeless it felt haunted.

Or maybe his definition of fun had changed since his injury. Being able to drive himself around was fun. Sex with Red was fun. Getting drunk with over-the-hill athletes and bitchy reporters was not.

Terra was still hounding him. Still using the guesthouse as her base of operations. He was trying to be civil. He hadn't completely ruled out broadcasting as a future. When he retired. Which wouldn't be for a while. Even though the pain in his leg screamed out a different timetable.

And when he tried to talk to Noah about retirement, about what he did with himself, Noah laughed him off.

"You said you had a business proposition," Tag reminded him.

"It's the week before Mardi Gras. Nobody talks business. I thought you came to have fun. The Krewe d'Etat parade is tonight. You ought to check it out."

Tag was rethinking his decision to come to New Orleans. A good time, he'd thought. A month-long party leading up to Mardi Gras. In the French Quarter, no less. A place known for the bawdy nature of its celebrations. After his sedentary autumn and winter, a big drunken party had sounded like exactly what he needed.

Except he didn't drink a lot. He wasn't a partier. He had too much respect for his body to abuse it. His adventures were physical. Dangerous pastimes requiring his head to be clear, his reflexes quick, and his body in top form. Swilling Hurricanes on Bourbon Street didn't fit that profile.

And he couldn't see Red doing it either.

Driving back from Pain and Torture was another form of agony. A parade wound its way through the French Quarter. The people on the floats wore tutus, elaborately decorated bras, and colorful hats. Tag decided to call Red. "Let's go out to lunch. It'll do you good to get out," he said when she answered.

She agreed. Quickly. His mood improved. Red had that effect on him.

They arranged to meet a block from Noah's house.

Red was gorgeous in her long blue skirt. Tag was getting tired of all the gold, green, and purple swathing the city. The only color he liked that wasn't blue was Gems' teal.

"Where are we going?" Red asked as she fastened her seat belt.

"Out of the city. Someplace where we can have a conversation."

"We could have stayed in for that."

"Do you really want to be cooped up there?"

She hesitated before saying, "I think there's something weird going on."

"Weird? Honey, we're in New Orleans during Carnival. It doesn't get much weirder than that." He slowed down, then made a sharp right turn. "Or maybe it does."

SKYE WAS GLAD he'd finally made a decision about where they were going to eat. Her stomach was audibly complaining. The building on the edge of the swamp looked like a shack. The air smelled of brackish water and rotting vegetation. A hand-painted sign proclaiming Poppa Jean's was home of the best blackened catfish in three parishes. There weren't many cars in the gravel lot—three in the afternoon wasn't a hopping time for any restaurant.

Poppa Jean's interior was as basic as the exterior. A tired-looking waitress showed them to a table in the far corner. After Tag slipped her a twenty beforehand. "And two Moonsinger beers."

"God bless smart phones," Skye murmured. They would never have found this place without modern technology. She was glad to be away from the madness of New Orleans. Glad to be away from Terra Baldwin's lurking presence.

"I know." Tag rolled his shoulders. "Who'd have thought I'd turn into the guy who—"

"Respects himself?"

One of his dark eyebrows shot up his forehead. "I've always respected myself."

Skye grinned. "I've seen you eat, Gentry."

"I've eaten you."

Heat rushed into her face. Time to change the subject. "I found out something interesting this morning," she began. "Or rather, something weird."

"New Orleans is weird."

She couldn't disagree with him. "Noah Nash doesn't own the property we're staying at. Not the main house and not the guesthouse."

Tag shrugged. "So he rented the place. What's the big deal?"

"I don't think he rents either. From what the housekeeper said, he's as much a guest as we are." Saying it aloud didn't sound as ominous as it had felt when Selena had called Mr. Nash the perpetual guest.

"That doesn't make any sense. He called me. Invited me down."

"He reached out to me by e-mail. When I turned him down, he went to the Gems' front office to have them vouch he was a legitimate former player. I have a contract. With his signature."

Or maybe not. How would she know his signature from anyone else's?

The waitress returned with their beers. "Menu is on the blackboard," she said before taking off again.

"I had every intention of turning him down. I don't want to travel. I want to stay in Columbia and build my business there. I don't even know how he found out about me."

"He's a retired Gem. He's still friends with a lot of the players. Maybe they raved about your meals." Tag didn't seem to think it was a big deal.

"Who are his friends?"

Tag seemed surprised by the question. "What difference does it make? Me."

"I didn't realize you were close to him."

"I'm not." Tag raised his beer bottle to his mouth and swallowed.

"Then who else? Who would have raved about my cooking to a retired player?"

"How should I know?" Tag's eyes narrowed. His lips thinned and lost their color. "I think you're making a bigger deal out of it than it warrants."

Skye sipped her beer before she answered. "So you didn't ask him to bring me down here to relieve your boredom?"

"I'm not that bored." Tag slammed his bottle to the table.

"Right."

And Terra is here.

She didn't know if the beer or the thought caused the burning in her stomach.

"What bait did Mr. Nash use to lure you to New Orleans?"

"No bait. He's a friend. He figured I'd be at loose ends, what with not reporting with the other pitchers and catchers. Unlike other friends I allegedly have."

"Don't get snippy." Skye was not in the mood for any of his crap. No one could dish out more crap than Tag Gentry when he was bored.

"Snippy? What the hell kind of word is that?"

"One that describes you when you're acting like a jerk."

"Maybe we should have stayed at the house and fucked," Tag muttered.

"Did you invite me to lunch to snipe at me? I didn't accept your invitation to argue with you." She used a rough brown paper napkin to wipe the condensation from her beer bottle. "I'm as bored as you are."

At least when she'd been in Florida with the team, she'd also been cooking for them. There had been no reason to fly her into New Orleans a week early. No one ate breakfast or lunch, and everyone went out every night. Noah didn't need a caterer.

Another piece she couldn't jam into the puzzle.

She peered at the handwritten menu on the chalkboard over the bar. "The andouille sandwich looks good." Eating local, learning about regional delicacies was a habit she'd developed when her father moved her around the country. Books and food. The two constants in her life.

"What is it?"

"Cajun sausage. Probably not healthy, as long as I don't make a habit of eating it, it won't kill me."

"Sounds good."

"So what did you want to talk to me about?" she asked. She pulled at the napkin she'd used on her bottle. The wet paper separated. She began rolling it into little balls.

Tag swigged more beer before answering her. "You're right. I'm bored. I was bored in Columbia. Now I'm bored in New Orleans. I'm not used to doing nothing. My body is twitching to go out and do something."

"I'm sorry."

"My damned contract with the Gems prevents me from doing anything that might jeopardize my recovery."

"They have a lot of money invested in you."

"All this forced downtime is making me think crazy thoughts." His scowl told her he didn't like admitting it. Even to her.

"Crazy like what?"

"Crazy like"—his voice dropped—"wondering what I'll do after I retire."

She felt bad for him. "Did you plan to play baseball forever?"

"Now who's being a jerk?"

"Well did you?"

"Of course not. I've put money away. Invested it. Things aren't like they were in the old days, when players had nothing once they were forced out. You won't find any modern-day guys wearing plaid suits and selling used cars. Not if they're smart."

"So what do they do?"

"Some guys coach. Scout. Broadcasting."

"None of that interests you?"

He shrugged. "Not really. And who knows if I'd be any good at it? There are only so many jobs out there. Not nearly as many as there are former players."

The waitress arrived to take their order. There were only three other occupied tables. Life was even slower in Louisiana than it was in South Carolina. "Good choice," the waitress said. "Poppa Jean makes the andouille himself. Raises the pigs, butchers them, and smokes the meat."

"You would be good at anything you put your mind to." Skye said once the waitress was out of earshot. She stopped pilling the napkin and reached across the table to cover Tag's hand. "You're the guy who got the Gems to their first-ever World Series."

He grimaced. Withdrew his hand. "I'm not that guy. Not only that guy. I was just doing the job the Gems pay me to do."

"Well, if you don't need money to retire, then what's your problem?"

TAG DIDN'T KNOW why he thought Red would understand. Nobody would understand. He wasn't a hero. Lack of funds didn't play into any part of his restlessness. He just needed something to do. Preferably something physical. He was too young simply to give up living. Seeing how Noah was surviving had only drawn Tag's concern to the surface.

His former teammate was usually bleary-eyed. Soft and expanding in the gut. Hungover or drunk. Always looking for a good time but never seeming to have fun doing it. Numbing himself to the hideousness of life after baseball.

Watching Noah made Tag want to punch something. Usually Noah.

"If you hadn't been injured this winter, what would you have done in the off-season?" Red asked.

"I was heading to Patagonia to hike the Paso del Viento."

"So you travel. You like traveling?"

"I like moving. I like going to out-of-the-way places and pitting myself against their challenges. But being a tourist?" He shuddered. "I'd just as soon feed my left nut to a shark."

"Don't do that." Red feigned shock. Her lagoon-colored eyes widened. Sparkled with the wickedness she kept hidden from most of the world. Except him. Thank God.

Talking about him was making him uncomfortable. Red probably knew him better than any woman alive, including his mother, but she still didn't understand the core of Tucker Alexander Gentry.

"What about you? Do you like to travel?"

The gleam in her eye faded. "No."

"Have you ever been anywhere besides Columbia, South Carolina, Zephyrhills, Florida, and New Orleans, Louisiana?"

"Yes, wise guy. I've lived in twelve states. Do you want me to list them alphabetically or geographically?"

"Really?"

"Really. I've done enough moving for three lifetimes. I'm fond of sleeping in my own bed in my own home."

"And alone." He hoped. He didn't like the idea of Red sleeping with anyone except him.

"Usually. I like it that way."

"So why did you come to New Orleans?"

"The front office pressured me to cater Noah's Mardi Gras party. Since I'm still waiting for my season contract to come through, I thought I'd better comply."

"Surprising you went to spring training without a contract."

Her coppery eyebrows met over the bridge of her nose. "It's weird," she admitted. "I've called the front office a couple of times about the contract and have gotten a lot of doublespeak."

"Don't you have an agent?"

"Not everyone with the team is a big shot, Big Shot. My work isn't complicated."

The waitress served their sandwiches. Tag waited until they were alone again before he commented.

"You will get the catering contract. You know that."

"I know." Could she sound any more miserable about it?

"You don't sound happy." He bit into his sandwich. Highly seasoned hot grease filled his mouth. He reached for a napkin.

"I'd rather have gotten the job on my merits," she said. "And I worry Dixon is going to hurt someone else."

She was referring to the blackmail video Tag's night nurse had taken of the team's majority shareholder, Drake Dixon, bullying both Tag and Red on Halloween night. Of Dixon wearing only a mask and intimidating Red. Of threatening to trade Tag to Japan. If that video ever went public, Dixon could be in a shitload of trouble. One of Tag's conditions for not posting the footage on the Internet or turning it over to the authorities was a guarantee that Red's catering contract with the Gems would be renewed. Tag thought of the video as insurance. His agent called it blackmail.

"You did get the job on merit last year. You shouldn't have to prove anything else."

"Can we change the subject?" Red sounded unhappy. As unhappy as he felt.

"Sure. "

Except maybe they didn't have anything to talk about. They couldn't talk about the Gems because they were still in the pre-season. And Tag didn't know if he wanted to talk about the team. Because the team might not be his future.

"So why did you move around so much?" he asked, remembering the twelve-states comment.

"My father changed jobs a lot, especially after my mom died."

"I grew up on a farm. We never even took vacations." How he'd hated the narrowness of that world.

"Next door to Christi Fellows." Red bit into her sandwich. Grease spurted.

He waggled his eyebrows as he handed her a rough brown paper napkin. "Good old Christi Fellows."

Red swallowed. "You know I don't believe a word of what you told me about her. Or your brothers."

"You can ask them."

"Do they come to a lot of games? Or are they still stuck on the farm?"

"No and no. The farm got bought out by one of those big corporations. My folks were smart enough to dump it before they lost it. Good thing none of us wanted it. Hunter is an aerospace engineer. I think he's working on a project to land a man on Venus or something like that. Cooper is a surgeon whose specialty is breast augmentation and reduction."

Red rolled her eyes. "Right."

"Don't mock my family." Tag struggled to keep a straight face.

"Don't you have a couple of sisters?"

"Piper and Harper. Both married. With rug rats. They were boring when we were growing up. They're boring now."

Red lowered her eyelids. Peered at him through her lashes. "That's not what Christi Fellows' brothers said."

The beer Tag had started to swallow spurted out of his nose.

"That was low, Red. Even for you. Christi Fellows didn't have any brothers." He paused. "Lots of cousins, though. They used to hang around a lot. Do you suppose my sisters... Nah. My sisters were boring.

Christi, on the other hand, was not. Did I ever tell you about the time we were all at the homecoming game at high school?"

"I wouldn't believe a word of it."

"Would I lie to you?"

"Like a rug, Gentry. Like a cheap rag rug." She grinned at him, which went through him like a bat slicing air on the third strike.

"Noah told me he had a business proposition." The moment he said it, he regretted admitting it. Even to Red. Who wasn't out to get him. "When I saw Terra, I thought maybe it had something to do with a broadcasting job. I could do that while I'm rehabbing. Announce home games."

Thank God there was no pity on Red's face. No pity, but no excitement either. "You could. I'll bet your voice would be real good for that. Did he give you any idea what the opportunity is about?"

Tag shook his head. "And when I ask him, he brushes me off. Tells me it's Mardi Gras. Tells me it's party time. Except he should know me better than that. I don't party. I never have."

As soon as he got it out, he felt better. Red wouldn't betray him.

"My father spent the last years of his life following random promises."

What did her father have to do with him?

"Don't agree to anything until you know what you'd be getting into."

"I'm not stupid." Why wasn't she commiserating with him?

"You're one of the least stupid people I know. But I think you're so worried about life after baseball you might miss the details from focusing too hard on the big picture."

"Don't judge me."

Red dropped the end of her roll to her plate. "No judging, Tag. But my gut is telling me something is very wrong here. You and I were both brought to a house party by someone who the housekeeper says is another guest. Your—Terra Baldwin, who's been linked to you in the past, is also here. But there is no need for a caterer because nobody here eats. When I try to corner my alleged customer about his Mardi Gras event, he doesn't know a thing about what he wants. I'm starting to doubt there really is a party. You try to talk to him about the business proposition he lured you with, and he tries to get you drunk. Like I said. You're one of the least stupid people I know."

"You're creating drama about a bunch of drunks who don't deserve your time."

She wiped her hands on an already bedraggled napkin. Wouldn't meet his gaze. "I'm ready to leave."

Skye stared out the window of Tag's rented car as he drove them back to New Orleans. The dreary, swampy landscape matched her mood. Lunch had been good only because it showed her why loving Tag or someone like him would be a disaster.

She was so sick of Tag's...whining. Okay, so he was having a career crisis. An identity crisis. Why did men have to get so tangled up in what they were instead of who they were?

Like her father.

I'm a salesman. I need a job that lets me sell.

How many times in her life had she heard that one? Right before every move, for sure. Probably dozens of other times before he found the next temporarily perfect job. Why couldn't he have been content to be her father? Or at least taken being her father into consideration before he made half-assed decisions?

Tag didn't make any attempts at conversation either.

Something was wrong. She knew it. Tag knew it. He was ignoring it. She was going to pack her bags and go home. Coming to New Orleans had been a mistake. Noah would have to find someone else to prepare all those lovely purple, green, and yellow peppers; the blueberries, green grapes, and pineapple she'd already purchased.

Tag dropped her off in front of the main house and went in search of parking. Skye hurried through the house and courtyard. She probably wouldn't have any problem booking a flight out. Incoming flights would be the jammed ones.

She might be the only person in the world who fled New Orleans right before Mardi Gras.

And that was okay. She was still true to Skye Schuyler.

She let herself into the guesthouse. And ran into Terra before reaching the sanctuary of her room. Or, more precisely, she ran into the cloud of perfume in which Terra was walking. Something heavy on the floral notes.

"You're in a hurry." Terra's languorous smile seemed innocent enough. "Rushing out to meet Tag?"

"Actually, I just had lunch with him." Skye was so distracted she didn't censor her words or protest when Terra followed her.

"He's quite the lover, isn't he? At least, he was before his unfortunate injury. Has it impeded him?"

"I wouldn't know."

Tag had never made love to her. They were fuck buddies. Were being the operative verb.

She was done. Finished. If she ever saw him at the ballpark, she was going back to the simple smile she'd given him the first season.

Terra laughed. "You wouldn't know? Come on, Skye. I might have been a bit tipsy the other night, but I know what I saw."

"You saw sex, Terra. And as I'm sure you remember, Tag is more than proficient when it comes to sex." Skye pulled her suitcase out of the armoire.

"Even with his leg in a cast?"

Skye hoisted the suitcase to the mattress. "I don't discuss personal business."

Terra plopped next to the suitcase. "His injury is more along the lines of business. Professional. Rumor has it there was more than a compound tibial fracture."

"I don't have a medical background. I'm the caterer, remember? And you'll have to excuse me. I have a family emergency and need to fly home." The lie came so easily Skye didn't realize she'd said it aloud. *Me, myself, and I. That's my family. Ever since my mother died.*

"What a shame. These parties are always a fun time. I was fortunate enough this year to time the story I'm working on with the Mardi Gras party."

Skye opened her top bureau drawer and snatched up a fistful of underclothes. And saw the manila envelope Tag had given her for safekeeping.

"You're working on a story?" Odd. The only thing Skye had seen Terra do was party or try to home in on Tag's sex life.

Terra laughed. "People don't understand that being a reporter is more than just standing in front of a camera and reading the prompter. There's a lot of background research and fact finding that goes on before a story ever hits the air."

Terra had just admitted she was working. Maybe Tag wasn't being paranoid about his medical records.

"I know what you mean. People eat my food, but they don't re-alize how early in the morning I have to get up to go to the market to purchase the freshest ingredients or how I modify my menus to accommodate what's available."

"I never thought of it like that," Terra said.

"Or how much research I do," Skye continued.

She wanted to keep Terra busy until Tag showed up so she could pass the envelope back to him. Terra's perfume was giving Skye a headache, but that was a small sacrifice to make.

"For example. I know next to nothing about Mardi Gras, so I got on the Internet to see what I should make for the party. I decided to go with the colors of the festival. Green, purple, and gold. You should see the bell peppers I got for a salad. It's going to be stunning."

Except she wasn't going to be making a bell pepper salad. Unless she made one in Columbia.

Terra laughed. "I don't think about food in quite those terms. Do you have your mask for the party?"

"I doubt I'll be back in time for the party. Besides, I'm the caterer, not one of the guests."

"But Drake likes everyone to dress up and wear masks at his parties."

Drake?

"You mean Noah. Noah Nash hired me to cater his party."

"Oops. My bad. Of course I meant Noah."

Liar.

Blood abandoned Skye's brain. The room tilted like a carnival ride. She thought she was going to be sick. Gripping the edge of the bureau helped. So did a couple of deep breaths. Until her lungs filled with Terra's perfume. Then she thought she might suffocate.

She had to let Tag know. Drake Dixon was behind their invitations to New Orleans. That could not be a good thing. For either of them.

"I've wanted to try your food since I first heard about it." Terra rambled on without an obvious destination.

"And when was that?" Skye released the bureau and began refolding her underwear. One way to disguise her trembling hands. She strained to hear Tag come into the guesthouse.

"Tag mentioned the clubhouse meals had gotten a lot better with the new caterer."

"I didn't know you were interested in food." Skye tried to keep her tone noncommittal. "Doesn't the camera add ten pounds?"

"Exactly. But Tag said you were feeding the players lean proteins and lots of vegetables, and it was all edible. That's so rare."

It wasn't at all rare. Terra was sucking up. Or detaining Skye for some reason.

"And I saw the shrimp brain at Drake's Halloween party."

It was a good thing Skye was folding panties and not something fragile and destructible. Her numb fingers couldn't grasp anything.

"And the asparagus fingers and radish eyeballs. So clever! So healthy."

Skye's throat tightened. "I had a lot of fun with Halloween." Until Dixon had tried to force her to join his orgy.

"I really can't wait to see what you do for Fat Tuesday. You're probably the only caterer in the world who could pull off making a last indulgence healthy."

"Terra, would you excuse me? I need to book my flight. Call a cab. Finish packing. And I'm not very good company. Terribly worried about my family." At least her alleged family troubles excused the shaking in her voice.

"I hope your emergency is nothing too serious."

"I won't know until I get there and see for myself."

"Of course. Let me know if there's anything I can do." Terra spoke with warmth.

Maybe she was nice person. Skye didn't know. She'd been too jealous of her past with Tag to give the woman a fair chance. She certainly sounded sincere.

Then Skye was alone. She waited until she heard the guesthouse door open and close until checking the hall to make sure Terra really was not hanging around, researching her story.

Empty in both directions.

Skye's fingers shook as she punched in Tag's phone number on her cell phone.

He didn't answer.

"It's Skye," she said to his voice mail. "I just learned Drake Dixon might be behind our invitations to New Orleans. I thought you'd want to know."

Then she called the airline.

FRIDAY, FEBRUARY 24 (CONTINUED) — KREWE D'ETAT PARADE

Tag's phone vibrated against his thigh. He pulled it out of his pocket. Red. He didn't feel like talking to her again. He was a little pissed at her.

She had no right to wiggle around inside his brain, steal his thoughts, and then spew them back at him in a logical manner. Or have the nerve to be annoyed at him.

He couldn't call her anyway. He needed to pay attention to his driving. Each day saw the streets more congested with tourists and other partiers. And the crowds only thickened as the hours advanced. Already people were wearing elaborate masks, which had to limit their peripheral vision. And it seemed like every time he turned around, another group—another krewe—was throwing a parade. By full dark, he probably wouldn't be able to get back to the French Quarter, much less find an available parking spot.

He circled the Quarter for what felt like an hour before a spot opened. He barely beat a black SUV to the gap. A white middle finger waved at him from the partially lowered dark-tinted window. "Back at ya, buddy," he muttered.

Just because he'd found a parking spot didn't mean he had to return to the guesthouse. Or the main house. Or any part of Noah's whacky weekend. He pulled his jacket collar closer to his neck. The air was brisk. Maybe cold enough to substitute for the shower he needed. He'd just walk for a bit more. Blend into the crowd.

The crazy crowd. Mardi Gras was still two days away. He couldn't imagine anything wilder than he was already seeing. Tonight seemed more like Halloween, what with all the skeletons wandering the streets.

But walking wasn't going to be an option. The pain in his leg, probably cramps from all the driving, barely allowed him to breathe. And he'd left his damn walking stick in the car. The cane Red had given him, with the teal pinstripe detail.

"Tag! There you are."

Noah, Terra, and another couple were strolling toward him.

"Where's your pretty lady?" Noah asked when he was closer.

Tag could smell the alcohol fumes wafting from Noah's mouth from at least five feet away.

They were still better than whatever Terra had marinated herself in.

"Didn't I tell you?" Terra sounded slightly smug. "She has a family emergency and is leaving."

"What? She can't leave." Noah's too careful enunciation only drew attention to his condition. "She has to cater the big party. The costume ball. She's spent a ton of money on the food already."

Noah's words didn't register, but Terra's did. Because Tag knew Red didn't have a family. The little clues she'd shared revealed enough for him to know she was alone in the world. Not that he cared. But he did wonder why she'd lied.

To Terra. Which was explanation enough if one thought about it.

Besides. Red wasn't his problem. Her family emergency wasn't his problem.

He remembered the phone call from her he hadn't picked up and felt like a shit. She was all alone, had reached out to him, and he had snubbed her.

"Excuse me," he said, turning away from the group.

Noah ignored him. "Hey, you remember Tripp Shaneybrook? Played for the Gems about ten years ago? Now retired. Well, look who showed up for Mardi Gras? With his wife, Kelsey. Tripp, Kelsey, this miserable son of a bitch is Tag Gentry, hero of this year's World Series, without ever playing in a World Series game."

Tag curled his fingers around his cell phone instead of Noah's neck.

"Chelsea," Shaneybrook said. "My wife's name is Chelsea."

"Excuse me," Tag said again. He pulled the phone from his pocket and looked at the screen. Red had left a message. He was punching in the code to access his voice mail when he saw a taxi pull up in front of Noah's house.

He pocketed the phone without listening to the message. The front door opened and Red stepped out, suitcase rolling behind her.

"Hey!" He limped toward her, every step generating a shaft of agony.

She paused. Waited for him to reach her.

"Terra said you have a family emergency."

She grimaced. "I moved your medical records," she said in a low voice.

He'd forgotten about those.

"You don't have a family," he reminded her in the same tone. "Are you running away from me?"

"Don't flatter yourself, Gentry. I'm running away from Drake Dixon. Didn't you listen to my message? He's the one behind our invitations."

Impossible. Dixon wasn't that stupid. "The housekeeper gossiping again?"

"No. Your ex. If you'll excuse me, I have a plane to catch." She turned to the cab.

"Skye! Skye!" Noah had followed Tag. "You have to meet Tripp and Kelsey Shaneybrook. We just ran into them. Tripp and I played for the Gems back in the day. Tripp, Kelsey, this is Skye's the Limit. She is the best caterer in all New Orleans. You have to come to my ball tomorrow night."

Definitely already drunk and the night's revelry hadn't yet started.

Tag saw Terra kick Noah's shin. Saw Red stiffen.

"It's nice to meet you." She smiled at the Shaneybrooks. "I'm not from New Orleans, and I won't be catering a Mardi Gras party. I really have to get to the airport."

"I know who you are," the Shaneybrook woman said. "I'm Chelsea. Not Kelsey. You're the team caterer for the Gems. My brother-in-law applied for the position."

As if anyone gave a shit. Damn it. Red was leaving.

Tag watched Noah sidle around the front of the taxi.

Well, Tag didn't need Red around. He hadn't even known she'd be in New Orleans when he accepted Noah's invitation. He'd be fine with the Shaneybrooks, Noah, Terra, and whoever else was slated to attend the Mardi Gras party.

Unless it really was Drake Dixon's party.

"Please. Excuse me. I really need to get to the airport," Red repeated and reached for the taxi door.

The driver took off. Peeled away from the curb. The stench of burned rubber momentarily masked Terra.

How much had Noah paid the cabbie to abandon Red?

"What was that about?" Red asked. "I need to get to the airport. I knew I should have waited until after sundown for Kahil."

"I can drive you," Tripp Shaneybrook said after his wife nudged his ribs with her elbow.

"I've got it covered," Tag said. "But thanks."

He grabbed Red's suitcase. He could appear chivalrous and use her luggage as a makeshift crutch at the same time. There was no way he was driving her anywhere.

"You don't need to help me," Red grumbled.

"I'm not," he replied in the same tone. "Don't you need to call your goldfish and tell it you've been delayed?"

If looks could kill, he'd be a dead man.

"Hey, we're going to get this party going," Noah said. He named a popular tourist attraction as a rendezvous point. "Catch up with us there. The Krewe d'Etat parade will be ending near there in a couple of hours."

Tag waved, as if signaling okay. The last damned thing he wanted to do was hang out in an overcrowded tourist trap watching a bunch of drunks desperately trying to have a good time.

"Forget it," Red said over her shoulder as she stomped into the main house.

"I didn't say anything." Tag was slower. His thigh felt as if one of his muscles was thinking about cramping up on him. Even the thought of the pain that would bring nauseated him. A hot whirlpool bath was what he needed, but he wasn't going to find one in the French Quarter. Maybe he could call Hector.

"I'm not staying here," she said as they passed through the courtyard.

"Where else are you going to go?" Tag asked. "And by the way, your cab driver was bribed by Noah to abandon you. You can try calling another cab if you'd like."

"Doesn't that tell you something? What else has to happen before you believe me?"

"Okay. Yes. Something fishy is going on." It galled him to admit it. "I don't trust Terra, though. Drake Dixon wouldn't dare try anything. He's not a stupid man."

"Terra told me she's here to work on a story. Called it a wonderful coincidence." Red reached past him to unlock the guesthouse door.

"Any hint as to the topic?"

"My guess is you. She asked a couple questions about your leg."

"What did you tell her?"

"The truth. I'm not a medical person, so I have no idea."

Tag opened her bedroom door. Stepped aside so she could precede him. He limped to her bed, released the suitcase, and collapsed.

"Tag?"

His screwed his eyes shut. Bands of pain wrapped around his knee, his thigh, and his shin. He couldn't walk another step. If the building caught fire, he was toast. And the nausea. As if the pain were a broom sweeping the urge to puke through his body.

Red's hands were cool against his face. "Are you all right?"

He shook his head. Regretted the motion.

"Is it your leg? You were limping pretty badly."

"Mmm." Easier than nodding.

"Do you have pain pills in your room?"

Red. She was going to take care of everything for him. Even though she was pissed at him. That was why she was such a great friend.

Someone had been through Tag's things.

Skye wasn't usually a paranoid woman. Except maybe when it came to Drake Dixon, when she had justifiable reasons. But this whole Mardi Gras mess was making her absolutely delusional.

Except someone really had gone through Tag's things.

He was compulsively neat. When she'd first seen his penthouse, she'd been positive it wasn't even furnished. But as she'd come to know both Tag and his setting, she'd learned he was neat and didn't like a lot of clutter. The foodstuffs she'd piled on his kitchen counters when she was cooking for the World Series or the Halloween party *cum* orgy must have driven him crazy.

Tag kept his shaving kit in their joint bathroom. She'd pawed through it just the day before, in search of condoms. He'd gotten testy because she'd displaced his dental floss or something.

Everything was now in disarray. As if Tag wouldn't recognize a jumble of items not of his own making.

She shook a couple of capsules into her palm, then turned the bottle to read the instructions. Except the pharmacist's description label of a round pink pill didn't match the white capsule in her hand. Not in color, not in shape, and not in size. She read the label again. *Oxycodone.* She recognized the name of the meds Tag had been taking in October, when he'd first been injured. He had to be in serious agony to request a pill now. He'd been overdoing it. Physical therapy, driving, walking. Rushing through rehab so he could get back into uniform.

Then something in the wastebasket caught her eye. Selena had already cleaned earlier, so the basket should have been empty. But a bright purple and green cardboard express envelope had been mutilated to fit into the container.

Skye returned the capsules to the bottle before pulling the envelope from the trash. It was addressed to Tag, in Columbia. From some pharmaceutical company.

That didn't seem right. Not that she was privy to most of Tag's life, but he didn't trust the mail, faxes, or e-mail. His neighborhood drugstore delivered to his penthouse all the time.

She opened the envelope and pulled out the packing slip. *Nandrolone-decanoate.* Her phone was in her pocket, so she did a quick Internet search to find out just what Tag had ordered through the mail.

The answer shocked her.

He was storing anabolic steroids with his pain meds.

She grabbed the edge of the counter to steady herself. *No.* Not after everything she'd done to get him eating right to help his healing. Tag wouldn't do that to himself. Bluto the Torturer, his physical therapist, had to be behind the shipment.

A peek into her bedroom confirmed Tag had gone to sleep without the aid of a pain pill.

Skye retrieved his medical records from where she'd taped them to the bottom of the vanity drawer. Yep. There was Bluto's phone number. Bluto's real name was Doug, who was just another victim of Tag's penchant for giving everyone a new name. If Tag ever became a father, his kids would be massively confused.

She dialed Bluto, letting her rage and disappointment dictate her actions.

"How dare you!" Bluto had barely identified himself when Skye let loose. "You put him up to it. He could get banned from baseball for life."

"Um, who is this?"

Skye inhaled deeply. "This is Skye Schuyler. I'm with Tag Gentry in New Orleans, and I just found the shipment of steroids."

"What?" Bluto's outrage seemed as genuine as hers, but who could tell over the phone? "What the fuck are you talking about? I do not put my clients on steroids."

"Well, there's a bunch of nandrolone capsules in his shaving kit."

"Not my doing. And if he's taking that shit, he can find another physical therapist."

"So what are the pills doing in his case?"

"Why the hell are you asking me?"

"Because you're his therapist." Skye wanted to believe him. She'd always liked Bluto. They'd worked together to develop an eating plan to help Tag's healing.

"Maybe the new guy put him on that shit." Bluto still sounded angry. "Hector Michaud is supposed to be a stickler about total health, which is one of the reasons I recommended him to Tag. But if he's got Tag on that crap, get Tag out of there. I'm serious."

"The pills were shipped to Tag's address in Columbia."

"Not by me."

She said nothing, her brain racing trying to come up with a reason for the steroids.

"Damn it, Skye, don't do this to me," Bluto said.

"I'm sorry." Skye's voice shook. "I was so upset when I found out what the pills were, I jumped to conclusions."

"I'll do some more digging on Hector. I don't like this at all."

"Thank you."

"Just so long as we're clear on my innocence, you can apologize with one of your organic carrot cakes."

"Okay." She disconnected the call. She should have known better. Bluto was not a pharmaceutical kind of guy.

What had Tag done with his pain pills? Skye went into his bedroom. Again, whoever had pawed through his belongings hadn't taken the time to hide their activity. Skye found the oxycodone in the interior pocket of his suitcase, wrapped in a plastic sandwich bag.

The pill bottle had said for Tag to take one pill as needed for pain, so she spilled one from the plastic bag into her palm and returned to her room.

Tag was stirring. Groaning a bit.

She perched next to him. "Still need a pain pill?"

"Half a pill. I don't like feeling all messed up."

Then why are you taking steroids? The question would have been so easy to ask, but she couldn't. Steroids were so opposite of everything she thought she knew about Tag. Yes, he wanted to heal so he could get back to baseball, and there were plenty of people out there who believed steroids promoted healing in the kinds of injuries Tag had. But Tag was a worker. He physically strained himself with Bluto. Sometimes Bluto had to dial him back because Tag pushed too hard. Taking steroids was almost like cheating.

Tag wasn't a cheater. So why the steroids?

Okay. She inhaled deeply. She and Tag were only friends. Nothing more. She could be disappointed by cheating, but not betrayed.

Skye carefully bisected the pill and gave him half, along with a glass of water. "Do you want me to put the other half back in the bag?"

"Bag? The bottle in my shaving kit. Right where you got it."

She shook her head. "I found your pain meds in a bag in your suitcase."

A scowl furrowed his brow. "I keep the bottle in my shaving kit. In the bathroom."

"There was something else in that bottle. And someone was in your stuff. Unless you've suddenly been cured of your OCD when it comes to your belongings."

"Are you going to tell me or make me guess?"

"Nandrolone. "

"Fuck you!"

"Not anymore." Her voice shook. She swallowed hard. "How could you?"

Except she already knew the answer. Tag would do anything to resurrect his career. Apparently even if it involved banned substances. She was just as disappointed in herself as she was with him. Her love shouldn't have blinded her to the extent of his desperation. If she truly knew him, she would have known he was capable of doing something as unethical as steroids.

"Wait a minute." Tag practically snarled the words. "How could I what?"

"Bluto isn't too happy with you either."

"Back up, Red. What the fuck are you talking about?"

"The steroids you had mailed to your house and that you put in your pain pill bottle so no one would be the wiser." Her fingernails dug into her palm.

"I'm not using steroids, and I'm really pissed you would think I would. And what does Bluto have to do with it?"

"I accused him of putting you on steroids. Of course, I apologized after he cut me a new one."

"This pain pill must have worked really fast, because I'm not following you at all. Start at the beginning."

So Skye told him about the pills not matching the description on the bottle. About the shipping package in the garbage. About the plastic-wrapped pain pills in the lid of his suitcase.

"Let me see your evidence."

She couldn't help herself. "I'll bring it to you."

He nodded. His complexion was nearly the same gray color as raw shrimp. He shouldn't have driven all the way out to Poppa Jean's. He probably shouldn't have been driving at all.

Skye fetched his shaving kit and the wastebasket.

Tag's hands trembled nearly as badly as hers had just moments earlier. "These aren't my oxycodone," he said as he spilled the white caplets from the bottle into his palm. "I've never seen these before in my life."

Skye handed him the wastebasket containing the green and purple pasteboard envelope after sliding the packing slip into her jeans pocket.

"I suppose you touched this."

"Why? Do you plan on calling the cops and having it dusted for fingerprints?"

"There's no need for you to get bitchy on me," Tag said. "Yes, I was thinking about it. Because someone is setting me up. I've never seen this envelope either."

She wanted to believe him. She wanted to believe *in* him.

His gray gaze latched on to her face. "Why would I risk flying with this envelope? Why would I bring an envelope addressed to me in Columbia to New Orleans? And don't tell me because it's easier to pack. You're a sensible woman. Give me a motive."

She tried to wrap her thoughts around his logic but instead remembered all the adjustments he'd made in his life trying to recuperate from his injury. Mostly changes for the better. But he was frantic enough to do something rash. Something reckless. Like steroids.

When she didn't say anything, he continued. "You can't. Because I'm innocent. But if you don't believe me, no one else will either."

Skye swallowed hard. "I want to." Such a tame phrasing of the fierce desire to protect him at any cost. So inadequate. "I really want to."

TAG GROANED AS he rolled off the bed. The agony choking his leg still hadn't acknowledged the pain pill. And the stink of Terra's perfume was embedded in his nostrils.

Red's hesitancy bugged him. If she didn't believe in him—and she was his best friend—who would?

"I will pee in a cup right now if I have to." Just like he did every day before physical therapy. Hector was a stickler.

"Not necessary." But her gaze wouldn't meet his.

"Steroids make your dick smaller. Why would I want that?"

Red snorted.

Thank God. Maybe he was getting through to her.

"Being a big dick isn't a compliment. And having a big dick? I've seen some Internet sites and think, *what would I do with that? It won't fit anywhere.*"

It was Tag's turn to snort.

"Those are the guys who need steroids. Not you." Her voice cracked. "Not you."

"Not me."

Red closed her eyes. Her shoulders slumped. "You're not taking the steroids. That means someone is setting you up."

If she'd sucker punched his gut, she couldn't have surprised him more.

When she opened her eyes again, they'd gone from sunny lagoon blue to stormy tropical sky. He could stare into her eyes forever and never tire of the weather.

"We need to get rid of the packaging."

We. She was on his team.

"Find a place to burn it. Or cut it into tiny pieces, soak it in water, and flush it."

"Burn it?" he asked. "Won't that draw attention?"

"We need to make sure it can't be resurrected. Burn it and flush the ashes."

"You have a criminal mind." Thank God.

"I read a lot." She pulled something from her back pocket. "Here's the packing slip. We need to destroy this too. But first we need to compare the amount of pills you have to the amount shipped."

He never would have thought of that.

He carefully counted the pills in the bottle. "There are twenty-seven here."

Red consulted the paper in her hand. "Thirty were shipped."

"I swear—"

"I know. You didn't take them. You would have seen right away the pills weren't the same as the oxycodone." She unzipped the large outer pocket on her suitcase and slid the shipping envelope and packing slip inside.

"I don't even take aspirin for headaches."

"I know. I shouldn't have doubted you. But who would want to ruin your reputation like this?" There went that maybe not so absurd allegation again: he was being framed.

"I don't have enemies. My career is on hold right now. The only person who would be worried about me coming back to the team would be Wes Dornan."

Wes had been the backup catcher until Tag's injury. Then he'd been behind home plate for every game of the World Series.

"What about Drake Dixon?"

Maybe Terra hadn't been bullshitting Red. Tag knew Dixon would love to destroy his career and his good name. It all had to do with a video Tag had recorded at Dixon's Halloween orgy.

"He's a possibility," Tag admitted.

Steroids could ruin him faster than being traded to Japan, which is what Dixon had threatened. On video. Naked. While molesting Red.

"You're injured. Lots of players use steroids to help heal. Someone might be trying to slip steroids to you and then ask for a test."

As if he hadn't already worked that out on his own.

"You don't eat and you don't drink anything I don't give you," Red said.

Which could get difficult. He understood where she was coming from. But she didn't go out with guests. Not to mention her plan to leave town.

"Do you think you've ingested any?"

"I wouldn't know. Want to check my dick to see if it's any smaller?"

Red narrowed her eyes.

"Okay, I'm being a wiseass." Maybe the pain in his leg was finally starting to ease, but he wasn't up—literally—for any fooling around. Not even an attempt. The most he could say was he no longer felt like hurling.

"I think we should get out of town," Red said. "Now. While the getting is good. Everyone else is out doing whatever it is they do. I can get you packed, get your car, and drive us to the airport."

It sounded like a really good plan. Except Tag still hadn't heard Noah's proposition for a post baseball life. And, more importantly, Hector the Miracle Worker wasn't ready to release him. Hector

Michaud's reputation was impeccable. His success stories might qualify him for sainthood. If his treatment could mend Tag's leg, Tag wouldn't need Noah's post baseball proposition. Of course, that was assuming the weird strengthening and stretching routines Hector had tailored to Tag's injury worked.

No, Tag couldn't leave. Not yet.

"I'm staying," he said. "You can take the car, though. It's turned out to be more of a hassle to park and drive than taking a cab."

"Okay. Now I know your pain meds have kicked it. You're not thinking." Red narrowed her eyes as if she were aiming X-ray vision at him. "Not with your brain."

He'd already told her the real reason he was in New Orleans. He wasn't ready to tell her the reason he wanted to stay.

"In fact, I don't think you're in any kind of condition to make any decisions about anything. Except the car. You're right about the car. Where are the keys?"

He groped in his pocket. Pulled out a remote fob. Dropped it onto the mattress next to him. "What do you want me to tell Noah?"

"Family emergency, remember?" She plucked the fob from the bed.

"Your goldfish get sick?"

"I told you. This whole setup doesn't feel right to me. The last time I felt this...icky was at Halloween." She tucked the remote into her purse.

Halloween. Drake Dixon's orgy. Tag had been there. He'd not only seen what Dixon tried to do to Red, he'd recorded most of it on his phone.

If Dixon really was behind her presence in New Orleans, Tag didn't blame Red for leaving. But Red didn't know Terra the way Tag did. Terra Baldwin would say anything if she thought it would advance her cause—which was usually her career. And after that little scene the other night, he wouldn't be at all surprised if Terra was trying to get Red to leave so she could attempt to repair her relationship with him. And by resuming their relationship, she might have access to his medical records.

But he couldn't tell Red that without sounding like a self-important jerk. He couldn't help it if women wanted to fuck him.

SKYE WHEELED HER suitcase across the courtyard and through the main house to the sidewalk. Tag's directions didn't make much sense to her. Essentially, he'd given her the name of the street on which he'd parked. She was on her own from there.

She asked her phone for a fake address on the street Tag had mentioned. Otherwise, she'd be hopelessly lost. She tucked the phone into her jacket pocket.

There were crowds of people in the deepening twilight. She wasn't comfortable dragging a suitcase behind her. Wobbly wheels fought for purchase on the uneven sidewalks. Faint strains of music reached her. There was probably another parade somewhere in the city. New Orleans teemed with them. She'd had no idea about krewes, their parades, or the other things they did for the city until Kahil the Cabbie—whom she should have called earlier—had enlightened her.

She hadn't paid attention to the Carnival schedule. What if she got caught in parade traffic? She was pretty sure she'd already missed her flight back to Columbia.

She was starting to see people in costumes. Bizarre costumes. If she didn't know better, she'd think she'd stumbled back in time to Halloween. Skeletons mingled with other pedestrians. Leering skulls clattered oversize teeth, adding to the natural commotion of the French Quarter.

Getting out of New Orleans couldn't happen soon enough.

She didn't see Tag's rental car anywhere. Was it possible he'd been in so much pain from the long drive he mixed up his streets?

The sounds of festivities grew louder as dusk shadowed the city. Music. People shouting. The horde of skeletons swarmed her. Engulfed her like a wave as they pulsed and ebbed, carrying her farther from where she wanted to be. To where the action was. One or two tugged on her arms. Others reached for the suitcase. She struggled, but there were too many of them.

She found herself on Canal Street. The parade was large and loud. Flambeaux carriers held their torches high, casting an eerie atmosphere over the already creepy skull-adorned floats manned by still more skeletons. The scent of kerosene or some other petroleum product wafted on the air.

The crowd was even larger than it had been when the horde had abducted her. Nearly everyone wore a mask of some sort.

She had to get off Canal Street. Back to the relative quiet of the Quarter.

Beads flew at her. She raised her free hand to avoid being hit in the face. Another hand, not hers, swiped the glittering purple strand millimeters from her eye. A gold strand hit her in the mouth before falling to the pavement.

"Mister, toss me something!" a woman behind her screamed. A blinking ball of light hurtled through the air. "A flashing skull bead!" the woman shrieked. "I got one of the flashing skull beads!"

Someone jostled Skye. She lost her grip on her suitcase. "No!" She stooped to retrieve it. Her hands groped between the closely packed bodies. "Excuse me," she repeated as she searched. She couldn't see a thing and relied on touch. And all her fingers encountered were other bodies. Some of whom, judging by the stench, hadn't showered in this millennium.

"There's the Dictator!"

"The Dictator!"

"I thought he was the king."

"Not this parade."

A foot landed on Skye's hand. Her cry was swallowed by the throng. Someone tugged on the strap of her cross-body bag, but she clutched it to her stomach with throbbing fingers. The suitcase was a loss, but a stolen purse would be a disaster. She needed that purse to make good her escape from the city.

She stood. Her luggage would have to wait. She needed to get off Canal Street, make her way back to where Tag had told her he'd parked the car. Find her sense of direction which had been consumed by the crowd. And still it seemed she was being jostled farther away from her destination.

"Mister, toss me something!"

The shouts never stopped. The pushing. The shoving. Green, purple, and gold beads bounced off her shoulders. The top of her head.

She might be pummeled to death before she could escape.

"Krewe d'Etat beads! See the bones? They look like little doggie bones."

How could anyone see anything in the dim light?

Skye stumbled over something. Big. Bulky. Boxy. She squatted again. Groped through the legs and ankles. Found a wheel and grabbed it. As far as she could determine in the dark, she'd located her suitcase. She latched on to the grip at the bottom and pulled it upright. It smelled of perfume, heavy and cloying.

Instead of dragging it behind her, she used the suitcase to bulldoze her way out of the crowd. As the mob surged toward the parade and the goodies being tossed, she fought her way to the backside of the throng. Away from the crush of bodies.

She was completely disoriented. For a moment, she thought she was on the wrong side of Canal, but crossing the street would have been impossible with the parade. The French Quarter was ahead of her. If she couldn't find Tag's car, she'd call another cab. The airport had to be less chaotic than this.

Someone grabbed her arm. She whipped the suitcase around, where it caught the masked figure in the side. He grunted. An oversize skull perched on broomstick-wide shoulders leered at her. Bony fingers reached for her again. Or were they beckoning?

She stepped back, keeping the luggage between her and the assailant. The *whoosh* of her blood against her eardrums was overly loud. The andouille sandwich from earlier in the day somersaulted in her stomach.

A muffled chuckle snapped her out of a temporary paralysis. Rage replaced terror. The jerk thought accosting women was okay? She'd like to raise her suitcase and smash it down on the mask.

"Skye." Hoarse. Barely audible above the din.

What were the chances of this…individual knowing her name? Unless it was someone from Noah's house party. Or Noah himself.

"Not funny, Noah," she said, her voice shaking. Her chest rose and fell with the effort of breathing.

Grinning teeth. Enormous, glowing teeth. Light from the passing flambeaux flickered against the giant exposed surfaces. The skeletal hand reached for her again.

"I've missed my plane. Tonight, anyway. But there will be others." Talking ramped her courage. She kept the suitcase between her and the assailant. "I don't know what kind of game you're playing, but I am not on your team."

Another chuckle. Vaguely familiar. Not Nash.

Drake Dixon. How could she have forgotten for even one heartbeat that Terra had slipped by telling her Dixon was behind Nash's alleged house party?

"Or maybe I should be asking why you're coming after me, Mr. Dixon."

She couldn't tell if the person under the costume reacted.

"Skye? Is that you?"

Someone, somewhere behind her, broke her trance. The giant skull had mesmerized her. But she didn't dare take her eyes off the hideous figure.

"Yes." She spoke loudly. Clearly.

"Are you okay? You're shaking."

Terra. Skye never thought she'd be glad to see Tag's...whatever she was. The other couple she'd met earlier was with her.

The skeleton allowed the crowd to absorb it.

Skye closed her eyes, but the image was burned on her retinas. And yeah. She was shaking. She used the suitcase to keep from falling. "I got turned around," she told Terra.

"What happened?" Noah's latest guest asked. She couldn't remember his name.

"I was looking for Tag's car and got swept up in the crowd." No one would believe her about being attacked by a giant skull. Which really hadn't attacked her. Which proved she was confused.

"I think Chelsea and I are ready to head back to our hotel," the new guest said. "It's been a long day for us. Would you like us to walk you to Noah's house?"

"Yes. Thank you. If it's no trouble." If she could walk. Her legs were as steady as pudding.

"Let me help you with your suitcase."

He reached for the handle, but Skye jerked away.

"No. Really. That's okay." She needed the suitcase to prop her upright. "I've got it. But thanks."

"Tripp," the woman murmured, perhaps cautioning him.

Right. Tripp and Chelsea Shaneybrook. Former Columbia Gem and his wife.

Skye needed to sit. Needed to gather her thoughts and remake her plans. She'd be safe with the Shaneybrooks. Maybe.

"What happened?" Noah caught up with the rest of his house party. "Skye! Glad you decided to join us. Let's get this party going. Where's Tag?"

If Noah had been in the skeleton costume, he was doing a good job of faking innocence.

"I don't think Skye wants to party," Terra said. "Look at her. She's shaking like you after a three-day drunk."

"Let's get her out of here," Tripp said. "Noah, maybe we'll see you again before we leave."

"I knew you wouldn't desert me."

Skye adjusted the bag of ice on her hand and stared at Tag, who was still sprawled across her bed. "Not everything is about you."

Oh Tag was involved, but whoever had hidden under the skull mask had said *her* name.

She flexed her fingers under the ice and winced. Maybe the stomped-on hand had been an accident, but she'd been corralled and delivered to a spot where that particular skeleton could harass her.

Someone had to be pretty devious to coordinate anything in such a mob. Which eliminated Noah Nash. He'd been too drunk when he'd issued the invitation for her to join his guests to be able to pull off something quite as precise as the parade incident had felt.

"I couldn't find your car."

"I parked on Burgundy," Tag said. He looked a little better than he had when she'd left for the airport.

"I couldn't find it. I brought your keys back. I guess I'm stuck here for the night. I'll call a cab in the morning."

"What happened to your hand?"

She told him about her unplanned foray to the Krewe D'Etat parade.

"I wasn't parked anywhere near Canal Street," he said when she'd finished.

"I'll look again before I head to the airport tomorrow." There she went, trying to appease him again.

"I don't want you to leave."

Skye stared at him. If he'd sprouted a third head, she couldn't be more surprised. "Why?"

"I feel...outnumbered here. You, you're on my side."

She opened her mouth to contradict him, but he didn't let her speak.

"Who else is going to make sure my food isn't spiked with steroids?"

"I'm scared." That was a good enough of a reason for her. She was tired of putting other people's needs ahead of her own. Maybe selfish, but true.

"I'll protect you. Haven't I watched out for you in the past? You and I—we're good at taking care of each other."

He had. Even wheelchair-bound, he'd taken care of Drake Dixon and his unwanted advances.

"Staying isn't a good idea." The thought of Dixon resurfacing wasn't the only thing that scared her. The intensity of her feelings for Tag weren't exactly comforting.

"I thought we decided a couple of months ago we're on the same team?" Tag reminded her.

"We are. But how often have you and a pitcher gone at it about what pitch he should throw?"

"I can't sit in my apartment. I'll go insane."

"How is that different from what you are doing here? I don't see you out carousing with Noah. And you're putting way too much strain on your leg."

"So now you're my physical therapist as well as my cook?"

"Not your cook. Your friend. I thought."

But he didn't believe her about Dixon. Tag knew what kind of hound dog Dixon was. Had even tried to warn her before she'd catered the Halloween party for him. Had rescued her from what probably would have been rape.

"Why do you have a bug up your butt about Terra's contention that Dixon is in New Orleans? You're the one who taught me trust my instincts. Well, those instincts started shrieking the moment Noah Nash had opened the door to me."

"Nah. That was me being here. Threw you off your game."

"I didn't realize you screamed soprano. Is that a side effect of steroids?"

"Funny. I wasn't exactly happy to find you here either, you know."

She knew. "No kidding. You don't mask your feelings very well. Yet we always end up in bed together. Why do you suppose that is?"

Tag leered. "I'm irresistible."

Skye swallowed the urge to laugh. "Irresistible? You're pathetic. You whine. I feel sorry for you."

"Are you okay?" He sounded genuinely concerned.

"I'm not sure." She wrapped her arms around her torso. "Probably. But getting caught in the mob at the parade—it was like Halloween or a monster movie. Skeletons everywhere. And I swear one of them was Drake Dixon." The dark, heavy, and dangerous coiling around the skeleton had been almost identical to Dixon's aura. Not that she knew an aura from a chakra. But her instincts. They were insistent.

"He's too smart to come near you again," Tag repeated.

Her temper hung by a thread. "Why are you discounting my words? Why are you ignoring what Terra told me?"

"You don't know Terra the way I do. She's a conniving, vindictive, and ambitious woman."

"So? I'm ambitious too. And none of that makes her a liar. Did she hurt your feelings?" Skye couldn't bring herself to ask, *your heart?*

"We were never serious."

"Just friends?"

Tag's eyes widened. "I am so not going there."

Skye curled up on the window seat, putting as much distance between her and Tag as she could. One of them had to have faith in her instincts.

"I'm going to book Kahil to pick me up in the morning."

"Please stay."

"Why?" All she needed was one good reason.

Tag hesitated before continuing. "You're the only person I trust here. You said it yourself. I can't eat or drink anything unless it comes from you."

"Don't do this to me." She could barely squeeze the words from her throat. Where was her survival instinct when she needed it?

"Invoke our friendship?"

There was a plethora of guilt stopping her from forming an answer. She owed him. Big-time. He had protected her from Drake Dixon's attack. He had rescued her and attempted to ensure Dixon wouldn't come after her again.

"Leave with me. We don't need to be here. Noah doesn't have a job offer for you. He's a pitcher. He's shaking you off. We were both duped into coming to New Orleans."

RED LOOKED DREADFUL. Her hand was bruising despite the ice pack she held on it. Her wild coppery curls competed with her clothing for the title of Most Disheveled. And she was pale. Her lips trembled. Her voice contained a quaver she couldn't disguise. The pain pill he'd taken wasn't giving him hallucinations. She was badly shaken.

And she was right. They both needed to get out of New Orleans.

"It's not just Noah and the job," Tag said. He hoped he could explain without sounding like a completely self-centered ass. "That's only part of why I want to stay. Yeah, when I asked him what he was up to these days, he said he does favors. So maybe he did invite me here as a favor to someone. A month ago, I would have told you he was a former teammate, not a friend. But why would he do Dixon any favors? It's not as if Noah is going to make a comeback or something. Maybe he was doing Shaneybrook a favor by inviting me. But I swear, if it was only about a job, I would be more than happy to blow this place and take you to Hawaii or something."

"If it's not about Noah having a job for you, then why?" Her gaze fixed on him, as if daring him to be reasonable.

The truth. He needed to tell her the truth. But would she understand? Could she relate to being desperate enough to try anything?

He took the plunge. "My physical therapist. The guy Bluto sent me to."

"The guy who makes Bluto look like a kitten?"

"Yeah. Him. Turns out he's developed a radical program for injuries like mine. Strengthening routines that make no sense but seem to work. He's the only guy in the country doing this. He's had real successes. I'm lucky he took me on."

She didn't say anything for what seemed like a long time. And when she finally did speak, she didn't sound happy. "Okay. You have to stay. But not here. We'll find you a hotel."

Right. Four days before Mardi Gras. But at least she understood. That meant a lot.

She looked around the room. "Did you see what I did with my purse?"

"You're still wearing it," he said. Further evidence of how upset she was. The strap cut between her breasts. Of course he was going to notice something like that. She fumbled at an outside pocket. The ice pack fell to the floor. "My phone." She dumped the contents of her bag onto the striped cushion next to her. "My phone." Panic edged her voice as she pawed through her belongings. "It's gone."

"Do you want me to check your pockets?" Tag offered. He was only half kidding.

"Not funny, Gentry." She squeezed her bag as if wringing out a wet cloth. "My whole business is on my phone."

"When was the last time you had it?"

"When I was using the map app to find your car." She stood and patted her jacket pocket. Her jeans pockets—really he would have done that for her. She crossed the room to where she'd abandoned her suitcase. The zipper jammed on her, and she uttered a curse he would have sworn she didn't know. She finally worked the zipper free, and more of her belongings flew about the room. But not her phone.

"Oh my God."

He didn't think it was possible for her complexion to get any whiter. He was wrong.

"The envelope and packing slip from your steroids." Her whisper was barely audible. "They're gone too."

"What?" He must have misunderstood her raspy words. Because it sounded as if she'd said—

"I don't mumble. I said the stuff I was going to take back to Columbia and burn is gone. How did anyone know they were in my suitcase? How did someone manage to open my suitcase in the mob at the parade?"

Calm. He needed to stay calm. "Is anything else missing?"

Red checked the inside zipper compartment in the cover of the suitcase. She methodically checked every cranny. Her hands shook so badly he thought it was a miracle she could use her fingers at all.

"Gone. The packing slip and envelope are gone."

Tag clenched his fists. If Noah were around, he could punch him.

She wrinkled her nose and shook her head. "No," she muttered. "Not possible."

"What?" Tag asked. Maybe she'd found—

"I thought I smelled Terra's perfume."

Someone else he'd like to punch. Woman or not.

He tried to focus on Red, not on the missing papers. "It's probably embedded in our nostrils."

That got a snort of laughter from her. "You're probably right."

He missed hearing and seeing Red laugh. Even when she was making herself crazy over things she couldn't control, he missed her. If he concentrated on her immediate problem, he couldn't panic about his own.

Her mirth faded. She sat on the floor in the middle of the room, surrounded by a messy pile of her clothes. "What am I going to do without my phone?" she whispered.

"You have it backed up on the cloud, right?" Even he knew enough to do that. He went through phones like she went through plastic gloves.

"I guess."

"So we'll go tomorrow and get you a new phone. A gift."

She'd opened to mouth, probably to argue, but he beat her to it. Red asked nothing from him. Wanted nothing from him. A refreshing change. He respected that. "Unless you have insurance."

She shook her head.

He knew she operated her business on a thin line of profitability.

"The envelope and packing slip are what worry me," he admitted. Keeping the strain out of his voice required effort. "How did your suitcase get away from you?"

She inhaled deeply, as if bracing herself. Maybe she was. "I was being jostled by the crowd. By people jumping to catch beads. I lost my grip on the handle. Someone tugged on the strap of my purse too. "

"You were distracted. Maybe intentionally."

"But how could they have grabbed the suitcase, open it, take the paperwork, and shove back into the crowd without anyone noticing? How did someone know the papers were in my luggage?"

He could guess. He might even put money on the guess. Terra ought to learn to wear less perfume, especially when she was lurking. "I'm more concerned that they're missing."

Red started stuffing her belongings into the dark teal suitcase. Literally cramming unfolded clothing into the compact space.

How she packed wasn't his concern. *She* wasn't his concern.

Except she was trying to help him. She was always trying to help him. Take care of him.

Part of him reveled in the attention, because she never asked for anything in return. Part of him rebelled. She was a force of chaos in his life, much the same as she was wadding her clothes instead of folding them. She brought disorder not only physically but really screwed with his head too. Because he wanted her. He wanted her in his life and that was messiest of all.

The zipper on the luggage wouldn't close. Kind of like the one on his pants. She had that effect on zippers.

"Come here," he said.

Her hands were still shaking as she buried her face in her palms.

She was all awkward angles on the floor. The jerky movement of her shoulders hinted at something he didn't want to know.

Red was crying.

Damn it. He'd only seen her cry once, when her server called in sick the day of the Halloween party. She was tougher than any woman he'd even known. Stronger. Not this...puddle. The parade must have done more of a number on her than he'd realized.

He was going to have to go to her. He sat up. The room wavered. Lurched once or twice. He paused, waiting for things to steady. When they had, Red was still sobbing. Silently. Which was somehow worse than if she wailed.

He swung his feet to the floor. The pain pill was definitely making him woozy. Slowly, he made his way to her. Somehow managed to ignore the agony in his leg to kneel next to her. Not a good idea. He sat and wondered how he would ever get up again.

When he put his arm around Red's shaking shoulders, she flinched. But she didn't pull away.

He didn't know how to comfort her. Wasn't even sure if comfort was what she needed. Comfort was an alien concept.

She turned. Dropped her hands. Buried her face against his shoulder. Clutched his shirt in her fists.

All he could do was hold her. He didn't know what to say. What else to do.

Besides, he had his own worries.

Saturday, February 25 – Krewe of Iris Parade

Skye awoke with a raging headache. She was curled into the furnace of Tag's naked body. They were in her room. In New Orleans. Part of the problem, she knew, was because she hadn't eaten since Papa Jean's. She had to be dehydrated too. Crying like Niagara Falls did that.

The details of now they'd ended up in bed were vague. He'd joined her on the floor. Held her. Somehow managed to get them both to bed, losing their clothing in the process.

She reached for her phone to check the time. Remembered she'd lost it.

Depression attempted to smother her in a dark, heavy, sodden blanket.

Tag stirred. Mumbled something.

There was still the matter of his missing rental car. Too bad she'd tossed Kahil's business card after she'd called him the first time. If she had her phone, she could pay him to drive Tag to his therapy session. But his number was now stored in her contacts, not her brain.

She eased her way out of bed. Tag's phone was on the night table next to him. It was still early.

She scooped some clothing from the floor, wincing at the mess she'd made. She wasn't as compulsive as Tag, but she also wasn't a slob. The tangle of her belongings was a sign of just how stressed she was.

Her face heated as she recalled the degree to which she'd given in to her fright. How she'd sobbed all over Tag.

Once she was dressed in jeans and a sweater, she started to repack, taking care not to disturb the still slumbering Tag. She hadn't brought a lot of clothes, so the process didn't take long. Her suitcase was more battered than it had been when she'd left Florida for New Orleans. Losing it in at the parade hadn't done the fabric any favors.

The larger of the two outside pockets had a long scratch on it, so deep it was only threads away from being a tear. Probably shouldn't put anything in there.

Once she had her clothes stowed, she tackled her purse. Its contents were strewn over the window seat. The cross body strap had been nicked, as if someone had tried to cut it. She started returning items to their designated pockets, still nurturing a hope that the missing phone was there, overlooked in her panicked search last night.

Nope.

She finished reloading the purse and discovered Tag watching her, his gray eyes dark instead of silver.

"How are you feeling this morning?" His voice was as rough as the black morning whiskers covering the lower part of his face.

"Embarrassed. Humiliated. Silly. Take your pick."

"Hungry? Or maybe I'm projecting."

Some of the pressure in Skye's chest eased. This was Tag, being irrelevant, and that morning, it was exactly the right thing to be. Her stomach growled in agreement.

"Lucky for you I can cook."

"I wasn't thinking about food, but now you mention it, breakfast wouldn't be out of line. I guess I missed supper last night."

"Meet me in the kitchen," she said. "I'll see what I can scrounge up for us."

Tag's leg still ached, but he had a physical therapy session in a couple of hours and needed to get moving. After his shower, he went to the main house and followed his nose to the kitchen. Green peppers. Onions. Whatever she was concocting, it smelled fabulous.

He took a seat on a stool at the granite-topped island. Red set a plate containing an omelet in front of him.

"No bacon?" he asked.

She arched her eyebrows as if to remind him he knew better. He considered himself lucky he was getting eggs. He sank his fork into the puffy yellow mass and found a garden of the vegetables she was always forcing into him.

"Maybe we should try calling my phone from yours. See if someone found it," she said, plopping next to him with her own smaller version of his breakfast.

He pulled his phone from his pocket and dropped it on the counter. "Knock yourself out. You're star four."

Her eyebrows soared.

Damn. He shouldn't have told her he had her on autodial. Because speed dial implied things he didn't want to think about, not to mention things he didn't want Red to know about.

Her mouth formed a grim line as she pressed the keypad. The color of her sweater was almost Gems' teal and looked great on her, clinging in all the right places.

God, he'd missed her knocking around in his kitchen. His living room. His bed.

A commotion outside in the corridor distracted him. The kitchen door banged open. Noah and Terra stumbled into the room, braying at some private joke.

Red turned her back on them.

"Oh!" Terra said. "Breakfast. What a lovely idea!"

Music, nearly drowned out by her enthusiasm, plunked in the background. Vaguely familiar. Some popular female singer with a throaty voice.

Red dropped the phone from her ear and turned to stare at Terra. Or rather, Terra's tiny purse.

"You have my phone," she said.

"What?" Terra swayed. Her overpowering perfume had been overlaid with perspiration. Makeup caked under her eyes. Clearly a rough night. Not her first.

"She found a phone outside," Noah said.

"It's yours?" Terra asked. "Here." She fumbled with her purse.

Tag didn't trust the gleam in her eyes.

Red sagged. She held out her hand. "I dropped it outside?" Her relief was audible as well as visible.

Terra slipped a phone not from her purse, but her blazer pocket.

Red stared at the device before snatching it. "Where outside?"

"On the front steps," Noah said. "Right, Terra?"

Red tapped a few buttons, as if to check for messages. "I guess it didn't break. I'm so glad you found it. Thank you."

Something was going on, but Tag wasn't sure what. He'd have thought Red would have been a little more enthusiastic about recovering her phone.

"I'm lucky the screen didn't shatter."

Not only was Red not enthusiastic, she sounded...wooden. But neither Terra nor Noah knew her well enough to pick up whatever was now bothering Red.

"How about some breakfast?" Noah asked, sounding jovial despite his bleary appearance. Stumbling in at dawn, sleeping away daylight—Tag couldn't respect that.

"Sure." Red didn't sound happy to be cooking either.

"Let her eat her omelet before it gets cold," Tag said.

"No, it's okay." Red strode to the refrigerator and pulled open the door. "It's the least I can do for deserting Noah so close to his party."

"What do you mean, deserting me?" Noah propped himself against the counter.

"We're leaving today," Red said. "After Tag's physical therapy session this morning."

What was she talking about? Tag could have sworn they'd decided to stay.

"But you can't go! We're having our own parade Monday night, and Tag is the surprise guest of honor. The King!"

"Good going, Noah," Terra muttered.

Red cracked eggs into a bowl.

"That's the stupidest thing I've ever heard," Tag replied.

"No," Noah said. "It's not. You saved the final game of the league championship series. You're the unsung hero of the Columbia Gems' World Series drive. We want to honor you."

Red's fork scraped against the side of the bowl as she stirred the eggs.

"I don't want it." Not only did he not want the dubious honor, he was mortified they'd even thought up the farce.

"We have it all planned, and we knew you'd balk, which is why it's a secret."

Terra rolled her eyes. "Good job, Noah."

"We're leaving after his PT," Red repeated. "And besides, it's not as if you know what you want for your party. You haven't told me anything. Not how many people, not if it's supposed to be formal or casual. I'll refund your deposit."

"But who's going to cook all the food you bought?"

Red shrugged before opening the refrigerator again. "Not my problem."

"No. I'm holding you to the contract." Noah was starting to sound a little desperate. "I'll sue."

"Oh that's the way to handle negotiations." Terra sounded disgusted. "Skye, I understand your frustration. Men just never seem get how much work goes into anything. Can I help you at all?"

Red's shoulders stiffened. Her hand trembled as she reached for a knife. Tag's angle was just right for him to note her white knuckles as she gripped the haft. He knew all about Red and her chopping knife.

"No. Thank you. I'm leaving with Tag."

She brought the knife down. *Thwack.* The scent of onion filled the air.

Noah yawned. His jaw cracked. "How long until breakfast?"

Thwack. "Just a few minutes."

Terra made another attempt at conversation, but Tag decided to eat before his omelet was cold, and Red seemed intent on her cooking. He knew she was more than capable of holding a discussion while prepping food, but this morning she wasn't in a chatty mood.

Butter sizzled in the pan, overly loud in the unnatural quiet. Until Noah snored.

The sound jerked him awake. His gaze bounced around the room, as if his eyeballs had become disconnected from his brain. Drool glistened on one side of his chin.

"Don't make Red cook for you if you're not going have the courtesy of staying awake," Tag said. He didn't try to hide his annoyance.

Noah started. "Right. Sorry."

A few minutes later, Red dished up an omelet for Terra. "That's an interesting ring," she said, as Terra took the plate from her. "What kind of stone is it?"

Terra turned her hand to look at the ring. "Thank you." She scowled. Picked a bit of lint from the prongs holding the stone in place. "Ulexite. It's also called TV stone. One of my first producers gave it to me as a going-away gift."

"Oops," Red said, bending down with a napkin. "Dropped a bit of egg. No problem. Well, the ring is really unusual."

Tag narrowed his eyes as he watched Red. She was up to something. That much he knew.

"Noah, your omelet will be ready in a few minutes."

He yawned again, without covering his mouth. "Sounds good," he mumbled.

"Oh this is fabulous," Terra gushed. She forked another bit of egg into her mouth. "I see why everyone raves about you."

Tag wanted to say, *It's an omelet, for crying out loud,* but there was no point antagonizing Terra.

No one spoke while they ate. Red scraped the remnants of her breakfast into the trash and started cleaning up while Noah and Terra finished their omelets.

Eventually Terra and Noah wandered out of the kitchen. They'd done justice to Red's cooking.

"What is it?" Tag asked as Red rinsed a plate before sticking it in the dishwasher.

She shook her head. "Later."

Skye locked her bedroom door, then checked the bathroom door he'd already locked.

"Why did you tell them we were leaving?" Tag asked. "I thought we were staying."

"We're leaving here, not New Orleans." She wasn't happy, but a hotel was a compromise that would work. "But first I need to check something."

She hoisted her suitcase to the bed. Next she pulled a crumpled napkin from her jeans pocket. She carefully unwrapped the contents and displayed a dark teal thread to Tag. "Got it."

"So?"

She placed the napkin on her suitcase, near the outer pocket that had been scratched. Looked like a match to her. Whatever was going on, Terra was in deep.

"What are you getting at?"

"This thread came from Terra's ring. It also looks as if she picked it up when she got into my suitcase at the parade."

Tag whistled. "That's why you wanted to chat up her ring."

"Of course. What do I care about her silly jewelry?"

"That means Terra has the packing slip from the steroids." The corner of his mouth twitched.

"Probably."

"So she could have been lying about Dixon being the true host of this house party."

"There's that."

"Or she just wants the story about me." He sounded glum.

"Maybe you should give it to her. If you give her the story straight, you're the one who would be in control."

"There isn't a story," Tag said. "I don't know what's happening."

"You know, she didn't find my phone. She took it."

He nodded. "Doesn't it make you wonder why?"

Skye shrugged. "Everything about this alleged house party makes me wonder. That's why I want out of here."

He couldn't argue with that. He held out his hand. "May I?"

Skye hesitated before slapping the device into his palm. He wasn't a spy for her competition. He wasn't going to steal her recipes or party plans and sell them to the highest bidder. She trusted him. "Knock yourself out."

THE FIRST PLACE Tag checked on the phone was her downloads. "Did you keep the video I sent you at Halloween?" The footage his agent called blackmail.

"No," Red replied. Her voice hitched. "What makes you think I wanted to be reminded of how naive I was? Or anything else?"

That was okay. He still had it. So did his agent.

The next place he checked was her photos. Red wasn't the kind of person who'd have naked photos of herself on her phone. Or anywhere else. He scrolled through pictures of food, pictures of decorations, and of brides, grooms, and Columbia Gems' baseball players. Nothing there that would prompt Terra to steal the device.

"Can I look at your e-mail?" He knew he would hate it if someone snooped into his correspondence. Not that he had anything to hide, but there was something about e-mail that was as personal as...underwear.

"You can look at anything you'd like. The only confidential stuff would be price quotes."

One of the things he liked most about Red. She wasn't wallowing in undercurrents. No murky depths. She was as open as a cloudless day in the middle of baseball season.

Nothing suspicious in her e-mail. In fact, nothing at all in her sent file. "How often do you clear your logs?

"I don't think I ever have."

"There's nothing here."

"No, that's not right. I was corresponding with the Jewish Community Center yesterday morning. I'm catering their Purim Festival in a couple of weeks."

He checked her text messages file. It, too, was empty. As was her recently placed call log. "Someone cleaned out your logs."

Red snatched her property back from him.

"I didn't have anything. Not even that Halloween video of yours." Her fingers flew over the keypad. "Why would anyone want to erase all my outgoing communication?"

"Think. Who have you talked to, texted, or e-mailed?"

"No one. You know what kind of boring life I live."

Unfortunately true. He was probably the most exciting thing to have happened to her in years, and that wasn't vanity speaking. "All work and no play."

She curled her upper lip at him. "And you're all play."

Which reminded him... He glanced at his watch. "I need to get going if I'm going to make it to PT on time. Where did you say you left my car?"

"Right where you left it. I never found it."

Damn. All he remembered was he'd left his cane in the vehicle, which meant he was going to be hard-pressed to find the car. Although he wasn't in as much pain as he'd been the previous evening, he didn't look forward to wandering around the French Quarter in search of his vehicle.

"Let me call Kahil for you," Red said. She found his number in her Contacts. "He can take you to PT and I'll try to find where you parked. It'll be broad daylight. What can happen?"

SATURDAY, FEBRUARY 25 (CONTINUED) – KREWE OF TUCKS PARADE

Not another parade. Skye heard the music—creepy, not festive to her mind—in the distance. She hated parades, believing them boring and useless and too crowded. She liked calm. She liked order. Parades were chaos. Everything that had happened since she'd come to the Big Easy had only justified her dislike. But as she'd told Tag, it was broad daylight and she wasn't wheeling a suitcase. She'd drive the stupid rental back to Noah's house and double-park if she had to.

Except she couldn't find the car. Anywhere. She wondered if it had been towed. Or even worse, stolen? Tag, being Tag, hadn't gotten a run-of-the-mill rental. He probably would have preferred a sport utility vehicle, but his leg injury prevented the climbing-in-and-out thing. No, Tag had to go with red. Flashy. Not that Skye knew much about cars. She drove a catering van. But she didn't see a single sporty red car anywhere.

She was about to call Kahil to ask him to drive her around the Quarter while she continued to search—she'd send Tag a bill for cab fare later—when she ran into Noah's friends from the previous evening. The Shaneybrooks. Tripp and Chelsea. They looked rested, unlike Noah and Terra had been at breakfast. They looked...happy.

"How are you doing this morning?" Chelsea asked. "You looked pretty upset last night."

"Upset is a good word," Skye replied. She didn't want to talk about the previous evening. "Tag seems to have misplaced his car."

"What's he driving?" Tripp asked.

Skye waved her hand. "Red. Sporty. Jock car."

Chelsea snickered. "There's a reason there are stereotypes."

"I don't drive a red sports car," Tripp replied.

"Before you retired?" Chelsea asked.

"Nope."

"It's a rental. I have no idea what he usually drives. He was probably so happy to be behind the wheel again after being laid up since October that he rented something impractical."

"An SUV would be impractical with his injury," Tripp said. "Why don't we help you look?"

But there was nothing red anywhere.

"Do you need a ride?" Tripp asked after half an hour of avoiding crowds stumbling to and from the current parade.

"I was going to pick Tag up from his PT session."

"He's still taking PT?" Tripp asked.

"Yeah." Skye's instincts said Tripp was okay, but Tag's injury wasn't something she was going to discuss with anyone. "That's where he is now."

"How bad was the break?"

"Bad, I guess. I'm a caterer, not a doctor."

"But you're friends with Tag."

"The team hired me to prep his meals when he was laid up last fall."

Skye stepped around a group of college-aged men who were making lewd comments to the women passing by.

"My baseball career—"

"You should talk to Tag, not me."

"Oh. I thought you two were together."

"Not really." Skye lifted her chin. "We're friends. Sort of." She wasn't going to admit to anyone that they were only having sex. "He trusts me."

And that was true. She hadn't realized it until she said the words aloud, but Tag relied on her. Maybe more than anyone else right then, including his agent.

"I don't have an agenda. I don't tell him what to do, except when it comes to eating. And I don't offer him career advice." She tried to smile in an attempt to take the sting out of her words, but she could tell she'd offended Tripp. She nearly apologized but bit down on her lower lip instead.

Chelsea snorted. "Tripp doesn't have career advice for him. He wants to hire him."

"Oh. Noah's job opportunity." Skye didn't know whether to be disgusted or disappointed.

"Noah?" Tripp sounded confused. "I wouldn't have anything to do with Noah Nash. He's in Drake Dixon's pocket and the only good thing about being forced to retire from baseball is not working for Dixon."

If Tripp had swung a bat into her gut, she couldn't have been more surprised. "So Noah Nash really is one of Dixon's flunkies?"

"I think Dixon has something on him. Noah never used to be a suck-up." Tripp shook his head. "No, I have this camp in Upstate

New York. For kids in bad home situations. Camp Home Safe. We use baseball to teach kids life skills, and I would love to have a catcher of Tag's caliber on staff."

Skye caught a glimmer of something in Tripp's words. "What makes you think Tag needs a job? He has a contract with the Gems. He's a catcher. Of caliber."

"I have nothing but respect for Tag. But I suspect he might not be able to return to catching. A catcher's legs are like a pitcher and his arm."

"He's working really hard," was all Skye was willing to share. But she knew Tripp was right.

"Of course he's working hard. If I gave you the wrong impression, I'm sorry. But Tag has to be thinking about the future. Questioning. I know I did when I hurt my shoulder."

So Tripp had been down the path Tag was currently treading. But Skye still didn't know Tripp. Didn't know if he had hidden reasons to approach Tag. She could trust no one.

"I'll pass the info along to him," she said. "That's all I can do."

"Fair enough." Tripp reached into his pocket and pulled out a business card. "Give this to him. Have him call me when he gets home."

Skye tucked the card into her jeans pocket. As she was turning to head back to Noah's house, something bright caught her eye. Something red. "What the...?" She peered into a narrow alley she had apparently overlooked earlier.

"Is that Tag's car?" Tripp asked.

"I don't know." Skye straightened her cross-body bag and stepped into the alley.

"I think so. You'd think he'd remember he'd parked in an alley."

"Wait." Tripp grabbed Skye's arm. "Maybe he didn't park it in the alley."

Which was when she saw the driver's window had been smashed, but no glass glittered on the uneven payment. "Looks like you might be right." She pulled the key fob from her pocket and checked the tag number against the license plate. "Yeah. It's his car."

It was a conspiracy. It had to be. They were never going to get out of New Orleans.

"Now what? I can't call 9-1-1. It's not an emergency."

Tripp already had his cell phone out.

"Let him handle it," Chelsea suggested. "He's good at taking care of things."

Skye started to protest that she didn't need taking care of but realized it would be a relief to let someone else deal with the hot mess of Tag Gentry's life. At least part of it.

She called Kahil and arranged to have him pick up Tag from PT, then texted Tag about the change of plan.

Tag glanced at Red, who was on her cell phone trying to find them a hotel, motel, bed-and-breakfast, or flophouse. Tripp Shaney-brook and his wife lurked while they waited for the cops. But the police force was busy. It was Mardi Gras. The Krewe of Tucks parade was known to be one of the rowdier events. A stolen vehicle wasn't a matter of life or death. It was a past event. Over. And it wasn't even Tag's car. A rental. A sporty red rental. Just asking to be vandalized or stolen during Carnival.

But Tag had to hang around to fill out the report. In the meantime, Shaneybrook was yammering on about the Baseball Hall of Fame and a camp in Upstate New York. A summer camp. Tag played ball in the summer. Shaneybrook hadn't been retired long enough to forget when the baseball season was active.

"Baseball as life," Shaneybrook said. "A catcher could teach decision-making skills."

Oh that was rich. "A bad decision put me in a cast and wheelchair for the World Series," Tag reminded Shaneybrook. Not that he was bitter. Much.

"Not your bad decision. You paid the price for someone else's error in judgment."

"So I'd be a living example." Burned coffee would have been sweeter in his mouth.

"No, you would help coach kids on how not to make lousy choices. That kid who mangled you? If you don't think he painted a target on his uniform for what he did, you're not the veteran player I took you for." Scorched coffee for Tag, sharpened spikes for Shaneybrook.

"I'll think about it," Tag grumbled.

"Your lady said something about Noah having a deal for you."

"Red's not my lady." Automatic. Without meaning. Except she was his friend. His best friend. Maybe more than a friend. An ally. Someone he needed. And wanted, not just for sex, but wanted around. Someone to hang with. And he didn't want to discuss Red with Shaneybrook. He didn't want Shaneybrook even thinking about Red.

"And yeah. That's why I came to New Orleans. Because Noah said he might have something for me."

"Word of caution." Shaneybrook hesitated. "Noah isn't...his own man these days."

Tag's head jerked. His eyes narrowed. "What does that mean?"

"It's Mardi Gras. Things aren't always what they seem."

"No shit," Tag muttered. His leg hurt. Hector could teach the Marquis de Sade a few tricks. But Tag wasn't going to take another pain pill. That much he knew. Yeah, the pain caused a haze, but better something he could fight than something induced by false means. Pain was natural. Opiates messed a guy up.

"You ever do steroids? To heal?" Tag asked.

Shaneybrook shook his head. "For me, it wasn't worth the risk. Are you taking them?"

Tag echoed the denial. "So what are you doing here? Did Noah invite you too?"

"I had the misfortune to run into him and that Baldwin woman. Well, not misfortune. I've wanted to talk to you but wasn't quite sure how to start the conversation. Wasn't sure if you weren't over your...anger yet. So running into you was good."

Shaneybrook surprised Tag. But Shaneybrook's bad shoulder had forced him to retire. He might be the only person in all New Orleans who understood Tag's frustration.

But he wasn't going to whine. He wasn't a sniveler. He was going to beat this injury. He'd be back behind the plate next season. Leading his team. Making those decisions Shaneybrook was talking about.

"We have physical therapists in Upstate New York," Shaneybrook said. "You don't need to give me an answer today. But think about it. The only thing on your agenda is PT. I'm offering you Cooperstown, birthplace of baseball, for the summer."

"Except I want Cooperstown forever."

Skye diced the beautiful bell peppers she'd purchased. Purple, green, and yellow: the colors of Mardi Gras. Wielding a knife helped keep her calm. The salad for Noah's alleged party would keep. Based on what she'd seen of him and his guests, they'd be too wasted to know the salad wasn't fresh. She had to do something or go crazy.

New Orleans was turning into a black hole. Or a rabbit hole, à la Alice and her stupid looking glass.

Once the peppers were marinating, she opened the refrigerator door to see what she could vent on next. Otherwise she'd start screaming, and if that happened, she might not be able to stop.

She was still in the kitchen several hours later when Tripp Shaneybrook slammed into the room. His wife trailed him.

"Where's Tag?" Tripp demanded.

"His room, I guess. Not my turn to watch him." She balanced half a red cabbage on her cutting board.

"Not your turn for a lot of things," Tripp muttered. "Take me to him."

Skye sniffed, thinking maybe Tripp had gotten into Noah's bourbon. No fumes. "Why are you acting so weird?" She plunged the knife into the cabbage. The crunch of the severing leaves vibrating in the handle was satisfying.

Tripp made a derogatory, animal-like sound. "I need to see Tag. Now."

His urgency was contagious. Skye dropped her knife. "Follow me," she said as she whipped off her apron.

They found Tag in his room, sitting on the end of his bed and talking on his phone. "Fine. Drunken frat boys took the car for a joyride. I still need a police report for the insurance company and for the rental company." He hesitated before ushering his visitors in.

"You know, I get that a stolen car that's been found isn't a high-priority crime. I get it. The insurance company doesn't." He listened for a few more moments before disconnecting.

"What's up?" he asked, a frown creasing his face.

"Have you looked at the *Sportsworld Insider* website today?" Tripp's terse tone raised the hairs on Skye's nape.

"I've been a little too busy to surf the net."

Tripp ignored Tag's sarcasm. "Check it out."

Tag brought the website up on his phone. He glanced at Skye when he was done. His expression was neutral. "I guess this explains what happened to your phone."

She didn't like the sound of that. "What?"

Tripp turned on her. "What?" he mocked. He shoved his phone under her nose.

Her eyes crossed, and she stepped back. "What are you doing?"

"Your name is right there."

"Right where?"

He did something to the screen on his phone and thrust it in her face again.

The packing slip for the steroids. The missing packing slip. Embedded in an e-mail. From her e-mail address.

"Those papers were stolen from me last night, along with my phone," she whispered. Her face felt funny, and tiny white lights sizzled in the air like water on hot oil. "How can this be?"

But she knew. Terra's byline was right there.

"I'M SCREWED," TAG said. And sick, deep in his gut. "Do you believe I'm taking steroids, Shaneybrook?"

"I think you were betrayed by her." Shaneybrook jerked his head toward Red.

"Really? Because she's the only one I trust." Absolutely. Red would not have betrayed him. Tag didn't have to justify anything to Shaneybrook—or anyone else.

"How can you pretend Skye's isn't involved in this?" Shaneybrook asked.

"She just told you. Her phone was stolen last night. She got mugged at the parade. You know that. She told me you walked her home. Besides, she has no reason to blow me in for steroid use." Red was his friend. His best friend. She believed he wasn't doping, and he was going to believe she wouldn't turn on him. He clung to that mantra, demanding it was true. "You don't even know Red. Don't criticize her."

Except the world was going to judge her. Because her name was on the e-mail. But he'd seen her face last night when she'd realized her phone was gone. He'd been there when she discovered Terra had it. She hadn't done this to him.

Terra, on the other hand—

Shaneybrook's wife placed her hands on her hips and tapped her foot. "Tripp, haven't you learned your lesson?"

"What?"

"Apologize to Skye." The wife sounded disgusted.

"But Chelsea—"

"How quickly we forget. Do you really need me to remind you?" Chelsea turned to Red and Tag. "My cousin told the media a lie about me, and Tripp believed it. He's such a sucker."

Color flooded Shaneybrook's face.

His wife didn't let up. "Tag *said* her phone was stolen. She *told* you the papers went missing from her suitcase last night. You *saw* that mob at the parade. Why is it so hard for you to believe a woman when it's not convenient for you?"

"This stinks of Terra Baldwin," Tag said.

Red's laugh was nowhere near believable. He knew her well enough to hear the whisper of hurt she was trying to hide. And that made him even angrier. She didn't deserve the damage about to destroy her world.

"Why would Terra Baldwin do this to you?" Shaneybrook asked.

Red tilted her chin. "I can think of a couple of reasons. Tag turned her down, for starters."

"I've moved on," Tag said at the same time.

"And he's her next big story," Red added. "Tag is a hot topic right now. How better for her to boost her career than betray a man she used to sleep with? It's a twofer."

"Could she be the one who set you up?" Chelsea asked.

Tag shrugged. "She's desperate for dirt on my injury."

"She doesn't have a story. She has a lie," Red said. She strode into the bathroom. Tag watched her rummage through his toiletry kit. Damn it, she was making a mess. She knew how much he hated anyone pawing through his things.

"What did you do with them?" She turned, hands on hips. "The pills. What did you do with them?"

"I flushed them," Tag said. "I don't want them on my person. You could have just asked, you know." Carrying steroids would be as damaging to his career as transporting heroin.

"Good. Did you rinse out the bottle?"

He nodded. Not even powdery residue remained. He'd heard everything Red had said about destroying the envelope and the packing slip. They should have burned the damned things in the courtyard, then flushed the ashes right there in New Orleans.

"What are you guys talking about now?" Shaneybrook asked.

"There really were steroids?" Chelsea asked.

"I found them last night," Red said.

Tag didn't appreciate her telling his business to the world.

"But they weren't his." She told the Shaneybrooks exactly what had happened. He looked skeptical; the wife, sympathetic.

"I don't give a damn what you believe." Tag could no longer contain his anger. He didn't care who he offended. He wanted the Shaneybrooks out of his room. He wanted to talk over this newest development with Red. Her clear-headed thinking was as good as his agent's, if not better. He scrubbed his face with his palms. Inhaled. "Look. I don't mean to be rude—much—but I just found out about this leak. Okay? I need to talk to my agent."

"Tell Marty I said hi," Shaneybrook said, as he draped his arm over his wife's shoulders. "I plan to call him next week."

Right. Something else he and Shaneybrook had in common: their agent, Marty Fiscoe. Another damned distraction.

Once he was alone with Red, he let his shoulders slump. Released the grip he had on his temper and other emotions. Like rationality.

"Now I really have to leave New Orleans." Red's strained control was evident in her voice.

"If you leave, people will believe you betrayed me. The only way to dispute that kind of talk is for you to stay. No one knows where we are. We can be anonymous."

She turned. Slowly. Her lagoon-colored eyes were dark. Stormy. "I can't stay. I have a business back in Columbia I need to tend. I...I can't stay here and pretend anymore. Besides, Terra knows where you are.

Where I am. There isn't another room to be rented in a hundred-mile radius. My only option is leaving."

"Terra is just jealous." Maybe reason would convince Red not to abandon him.

"Of our friendship? Of our fucking?"

He cringed. "We've got more than that. We've got a trust thing going on. I trust you."

"Thank you." Her quiet dignity reassured him.

"If we go back to Columbia now, the press will be camped at my place, at your place—we will find no peace. Terra is the only one who knows where we are, and she's already played her hand."

"It's all a ploy to keep us here. Together," Red replied.

"I'm not quite as ready to be as paranoid as you are."

Her answering smile was crooked. Slightly twisted. Almost broken. "Do you really believe drunken frat boys stole your car for joyriding?"

"The police said the Krewe of Tucks is an incarnation of *Animal House.* So yeah, it's not a stretch for me."

"Your car went missing last night. Before I could leave. Before the Tuckers or Truckers or whatever were prancing through the French Quarter wreaking havoc. I feel like I'm in an episode of the *Twilight Zone* where everything I do to try to get out of here is thwarted. Now you're jumping into the fray."

He heard words he'd never thought he'd hear himself say. To anyone. Ever. "I need you." Yeah. Those three words. Out of his mouth.

Red's eyes widened. Her lips twitched.

His phone rang. He glanced at the screen and grimaced. His agent's timing was a little off, but he couldn't ignore the call.

"Hi, Marty. You're on speaker, and Celeste Schuyler, alleged author of the damning e-mail, is with me."

"You sound like a talk show host," Marty responded. "Is she confessing?"

"Her phone was stolen last night. I witnessed her having it returned this morning. By Terra Baldwin."

"I thought you and the Baldwin woman were an item."

"We haven't been together since before my injury." A long time before his injury. But they'd never been serious. Or exclusive. Now Tag had to wonder why he'd been with her at all.

Convenient sex. Baseball groupies weren't convenient. Terra had been.

"I got people asking me about this Schuyler woman."

"I'm the team caterer. It's all on my website," Red said.

"Your relationship with Tag isn't," Marty pointed out.

"My relationship with Tag is no one's business."

"People are making it their business since you sent out this e-mail accusing him of being on steroids."

"She didn't send the e-mail," Tag said. "Terra is here, where we are, and she's jealous. And ambitious. If she can't get the real story about my injury, she'll make up one, and that's exactly what she did."

Red pulled out her phone and swiped at the screen a few times. Marty yammered on, but Tag watched Red too closely to listen. Her lips tightened. Nostrils flared. Eyes scanned the small screen she held. Her fingers worked. Her already pale complexion turned nearly translucent.

"So what do you think?" Marty concluded.

"What's wrong?" Tag asked Red.

"She put my e-mail address out there." Strain tainted every syllable. "People think I exposed you. Some people are glad. Others..." She sat on the end of his bed as if her legs would no longer support her. "I don't know if some of what they suggest is anatomically possible."

"What?" Marty must have caught part of that.

"Can I call you back?" Tag asked, his gaze never leaving Red.

"Sure. I know you two have to discuss the whole fake-engagement thing, so—"

"What fake-engagement thing?" Tag asked.

"Weren't you listening to me?"

"No. I'll call you later." Tag disconnected the call. He sat next to Red and took her phone from her icy fingers. Read.

Ouch. A lot of his fans weren't feeling kindly toward her.

"They don't know you," he said in a low voice. Being his friend was going to cost her. Unless he could do something to neutralize the hate. What had Marty said about a fake engagement?

"I don't know whether Terra was out to get you or me," Red replied. "Who's sustaining the most damage?"

"The only person who needs to believe you is me," Tag reminded her.

She nodded, ever so slightly.

"I believe you." Shit. Were her eyes so shiny because of tears?

Red was too strong to make a habit out of this crying stuff. She was the only person on the face of the earth who expected nothing from him. That made her the only person in the known universe he could trust. And he trusted her not to cry.

The teardrop didn't move but hovered in the corner of her eye like a threat.

"Fine. We believe each other. But that's not going to help expunge the scandal from your name, and it's not going to help me stay in business. Especially with the team."

"What do you mean?"

"Well, some of the guys support steroid use to aid healing."

"So?"

She held out her hand for her phone, but he wasn't finished reading her hate mail.

Ah. Not just his fans. Some of his teammates chiding her for going public instead of letting the team handle the situation internally. She was, according to them, a traitor to the Gems and a traitor to the city of Columbia and the state of South Carolina. Except they weren't quite so polite.

"All the more reason you should stay here with me."

"I have a big event on March twelfth. For people who probably don't care about baseball."

"I don't know. Everyone in Columbia loves the Gems." When she didn't smile at his admittedly lame attempt at a joke, he draped his arm over her shoulder. "Stay. We can protect each other."

"I don't need your protection," Red snapped.

"Maybe I need yours," he snarled back. What was wrong with the woman? Why did she continually push him away?

TAG'S WORDS SLAMMED into Skye's chest with an ache from which she might not ever heal.

He needed her? *Right.* Tag Gentry didn't need anyone. Or if he did, it was only to protect him from appearing vulnerable to the world.

She couldn't do it anymore. She couldn't be his buffer, his cushion against reality. Not any longer. It was time to think about Skye. Time to gather the pieces of her splintering heart and try to heal. Try to get over him. She needed to get away from him. She'd been doing so well in Florida with the team and away from his heartbreaking presence. Until she'd been railroaded to New Orleans. And once she was in proximity to Tag, they wound up in bed together. Laughing together. Understanding each other.

How could she not love him?

All she was to him was his current best friend. With benefits. And that wasn't enough for her anymore. She shouldn't love him for when she was merely an afterthought. But the heart didn't listen to logic.

She needed to go home. Get back into her routines. Try to develop new business. Her gut screamed that no matter how hard Tag pushed Dixon into renewing her contract to cater the Gems' home games, it was not going to happen. Not now. Not when the players and management believed she'd sold out the player who'd gotten them into the World Series.

She took her phone back from Tag.

"Terra is *not* going to win," he said.

"This isn't about winning or losing."

Tag covered her hand. His was big. Still calloused from catching baseballs. And warm. Overwhelmingly warm. "I wasn't paying much attention to Marty just now, because I was worried about you, but toward the end, I'm pretty sure I heard him say we ought to get engaged. And you know, that makes sense. We can show the world you didn't send the e-mail to Terra. That she's a jealous, vindictive bitch."

"Then what?"

"Huh?"

"Then what? Do we break it off after a few months because I can't stand that you're on the road so much of the year? Do I find you in bed with some sweet young thing in a hotel room in New York? And what if I meet someone? You know, a real someone. Or you do? Then what do we do?"

His mouth was open, so her questions must have surprised him.

"I don't want to meet anyone else." His eyes widened, as if he couldn't believe the words that had just come out of his mouth. She certainly didn't.

"You know, it doesn't have to be a fake engagement. We could, I don't know, be seen picking out a ring, being all lovey-dovey in public—"

"No." Skye swallowed, trying to keep her tenuous control. "We agreed last fall. Friends with benefits. Nothing more."

His mouth worked, as if he knew he wanted to say something, but he didn't know what.

"You can't go changing the rules on me." The best defense, according to casual wisdom, was a good offense. Skye hoped Tag wouldn't catch on to her strategy.

"I've changed my mind," Tag said.

Skye spoke the most difficult words she would ever speak: "I haven't changed mine."

"Woo!" Noah said as he came into the kitchen. The inevitable glass of whiskey sloshed over the hand holding it. The smell mingled with the yeasty aroma haunting the room. "We're going to have a party!"

Every ounce of Skye's willpower went into not making an acerbic reply.

"Tomorrow night." Noah's words slurred ever so slightly. "The culmination of everything, ending in my freedom."

Skye opened the oven door, as if the king cake she was attempting to bake required her immediate attention. The escaping heat blew lose strands of her hair around her face. She wasn't going to let Noah suck her into anything else. The fact she was still in New Orleans was a testament to her fear.

Tag had faced his. She needed to do the same. But not with a drunk like Noah Nash. He was a puppet. She wanted the marionette master, the string puller. And that wasn't Terra Baldwin, no matter how desperately she was trying to make Skye and Tag think so. This whole Mardi Gras thing was about Drake Dixon.

Dixon was out to destroy Tag because Tag had defended her. She was not going to let Dixon win. If that meant a faux engagement to Tag, well, she was going to have to suck it up and be on Tag's team. He'd saved her. It was time to return the favor.

She closed the oven door and stood.

"So what are you going to do to make this party memorable?" Noah asked. "Special."

"I have a feeling you can accomplish that all by yourself. I'm just the caterer."

"Oh but the things I've heard about you." Noah waved a finger under her nose.

"I wouldn't believe everything I heard." The peppers were diced and the cabbages sliced. She started scrubbing the purple fingerling potatoes. She'd mix in a few Yukon Golds, but the roasted potatoes would be primarily purple. Snipped chives would add the green.

Green, gold, and purple. Faith, power, and justice. Kahil had explained the symbolism to her as he'd driven her to the markets.

Faith. Power. Justice.

"What meats are you serving?" Noah awkwardly planted himself on one of the stools at the granite-topped island.

Faith. She needed faith in Tag. He hadn't given her any reason to distrust him.

"It's Fat Tuesday! It's our last hurrah." Noah started to slip from his stool but braced himself on one leg.

Power. Who really had the power here? Dixon had the power only if Skye and Tag let him get away with bullying them.

"Gumbo. Po'boys." Noah's voice took on a whining quality that irked her.

"I have been trying to get your ideas for the past week. And you want to talk about this now?"

"Jambalaya. Spicy but not too spicy. Don't want blisters on the lips. People might confuse them for symptoms of a STD. Wouldn't want that, would we?" He winked and raised his glass to his mouth.

Justice. Maybe there was no such thing as justice. She was stuck in New Orleans, wasn't she?

She picked up a sturdy fork and started poking holes in the potatoes so they wouldn't explode in the oven.

"You're forking those potatoes!" Noah snickered at his own bad joke.

Juvenile. She'd met a lot of baseball players with the same sense of humor in Florida. The guys who actually made their way to Columbia were more mature. With Noah, it was difficult to tell if immaturity, alcohol, or a mix of both was responsible.

"So why did you hire me? I don't cook unhealthy. That's my trademark."

"You came very highly recommended."

"By whom?"

Noah wagged his finger again.

She clenched her teeth to keep from biting him. "You're not helping. I need to know who to serve the piece of king cake with the baby in it." She hadn't baked a plastic baby, the custom, into the cake, fearing it might melt. Kahil could insist it was safe all he wanted. Instead, she planned to poke the tiny figurine into the cake before serving it. Yeah, there would be a gap in the icing, but the way this crowd caroused, no one would notice.

Noah's eyebrows arched. "Oh. Aren't you the clever one? Rig the king cake." He laughed. Or snorted. Skye wasn't sure which. "Tag is the king of the party. He should receive the baby. He can host the next party. But it's a surprise. So *shhh*." A spray of spittle escaped Noah's mouth. "Don't tell him."

Noah was enough of a drunk—or a dunce—to contrive to keep Tag in New Orleans because he was the honorary king of a party and not blink an eye about how that goal was achieved.

"I won't breathe a word," Clearly Noah had forgotten he'd already blatted out his secret.

"Tag is the king and Terra will be his queen."

Skye stiffened as if he'd slapped her. "I don't think so. He's not awfully fond of her right now. I'm sure you've seen the article she wrote. It's all over the Internet."

"And sports talk radio and TV," Noah agreed. "But you're the one who sent her the stuff."

Skye narrowed her eyes and watched Noah as he took another swig from his glass. "Even if I did, which I did not, she could have not done anything with it. If she had any feelings at all for him, she would have killed the story. No matter how hard you two try to frame me for betraying Tag, in the end it comes down to what Terra did with the information."

Noah flinched.

The oven timer buzzed. Skye grabbed her mitt and opened the oven door. Cinnamon and yeast twined into a welcoming fragrance. Judging by the aroma, her first attempt at a king cake was a success.

She tried to stand, but Noah had crept up behind her. Close behind her. The heat from the baking sheet was starting to seep through the fabric of her mitt. "Excuse me." Skye couldn't keep her annoyance from her voice. She hated having anyone around while she was cooking. Except Tag. He knew enough not to get in her way.

"Smells good," Noah said, far too close to her ear.

"Please move."

"Cake smells good too."

Dear God, was he sniffing her hair?

"No wonder Tag likes fucking you."

That did it. "I'm holding a pan which has been in a three-hundred-seventy-five-degree oven for half an hour. I would really hate to drop it on the side of your head."

He took a step back.

"I am not kidding, Noah. You just went way over the line with me, and if you don't back off right now, not only will you have third-degree burns on your face, I will sue you for sexual harassment."

"You can't prove anything." Bravado weighted his words, but he retreated.

She straightened and put the king cake on the top of the stove.

"I've had it with you." She was shocked her voice didn't shake. "I've had it with Terra. If Tag hadn't asked me to stay, I would be gone so fast. So let's get one thing very clear, Mr. Nash."

"I always heard redheads were feisty. No wonder Tag doesn't want to share you. Selfish bastard."

Skye reached across the counter and grabbed her knife. Holding it in front of her, she said, "I can bone a chicken in my sleep."

Noah's face lost some of its floridity. He stepped back. "You can't threaten me. I hired you."

"So fire me." She hoped he would. She prayed he would.

But he didn't.

Instead he turned and fled the kitchen.

Which confirmed for her that, despite signatures on contracts, Noah Nash had not been the person to hire her.

Red was leaving him. She wasn't going to help him by faking a relationship. Not only was she not going to help him, she was deserting him.

Tag sat on the end of his bed. His stomach was knotted tighter than the stitches on a baseball. Red was abandoning him to Terra. A terrorist.

He smirked. A good label for his ex.

Who let herself into his room.

He blinked.

Yep. That was Terra. Wearing...not very much. A guy didn't even need an imagination.

"What do you want?" he growled. He'd much rather be wallowing in his sorrow at Red's repudiation of their friendship than spar with Terra.

"I'm so sorry, Tag. About what Skye did to you."

He was not going to let Terra get away with framing Red. "She didn't do anything. You did."

Terra stiffened. "My editor needed a quick fill story from me. What was I supposed to do? Sit on the fact that you're using steroids?"

"Get out of my room. Out of my life."

"Please," she said in the breathless voice that had once, inexplicably, aroused him.

"The only way to please me is by getting out of my room. Now." How could he have ever found her attractive?

"Tag, I—" Red burst through the bathroom door. Looked at nearly naked Terra, then at him.

Uh-oh.

"I believed you when you asked me to marry you," Red said in a tone of voice he didn't recognize. And when had he—oh. Yeah. Something weird happened in his chest.

"Terra has a difficult time with good-byes," he replied. "Terra, if you'll excuse us, my fiancée and I have a lot to discuss."

He didn't want to stop looking at Red, with her wild coppery curls, her wide lagoon-colored eyes, her full lips, parted ever so slightly and glistening as if she were about to go down on him. His cock stirred.

"Now, Terra." He forced his gaze from Red to his ex. "And don't come back. You're not welcome."

He held out his hand to Red, who took the hint and joined him on the bed. Her fingers twined with his. Her hands weren't smooth or soft but nearly as calloused and rough as his. And he liked that she was more concerned about what she did for a living than appearances. Maybe she wasn't as adventurous as he was, but he respected her. Her honesty. Her integrity. Her body. Her faithfulness.

"You can't change the course of events." Terra's voice was low. Hissy as well as pissy.

"Neither can you. Get out now before I throw you out. I might be lame, but that's only increased my upper body strength. It would inconvenience me only because I would have to touch you."

"I'll take your word for it." Terra stopped in the doorway. Looked back at him. "For now."

He didn't release Red's hand. Even when she tried to tug free, he only tightened his grip. She smelled of fresh-baked bread and cinnamon.

"What made you change your mind?" He didn't know what to expect. He didn't even know what he hoped her answer would be.

"Justice. I was baking the king cake for the party, thinking about the colors of Mardi Gras and what they're supposed to mean, and got stuck on justice."

He buried his face in the crook of her neck. He never could follow a woman's logic.

"I owe you. If pretending to be engaged to me will help you, if you think we can defuse the scandal that way, then I'm in for you. That's what friends do."

Friends. He was starting to hate the word.

"And I had to threaten our alleged host with bodily harm," she continued.

He thought his brain would explode. "What?"

"Noah tried to—I don't know—intimidate me? I threatened to hit him in a face with a baking sheet I'd just taken out of the oven."

"I'm going to kill him." Tag released her hand and lurched to his feet.

Red grabbed his fingers and drew him back to the bed.

"He's not worth going to jail for," she said. "And he did tell me some interesting things. Like about tomorrow night's party."

"I think you're right." He had to weigh the consequences of not just his career, but of keeping Red in his life. "I've changed my mind too. We need to get out of New Orleans."

"You're the guest of honor at Noah's party. The king. In Mardi Gras parlance, that's a big deal."

As if he cared about stupid things like traditions of a place he'd never seen before and probably would never visit again.

"You're the king, and Terra is slated to be your queen." Her usually plump lips thinned into a harsh line.

"Over my dead body."

"Yeah, and since I'm not quite done with your body, I'm not liking the dead part."

That stung. A little. He was more than a body. Maybe he and Red needed to redefine their relationship. Lots had changed since the World Series. Including him.

"You're my queen."

"Damn right."

"Let's go pick out a ring today."

"We don't need to get carried away," she said. "Just a public proposal tomorrow night at the party."

Carried away? How was putting an engagement ring on her finger getting carried away? The more he thought about getting married to Red, the more he liked the idea. The sex was good. He enjoyed her company. She made him laugh. She wasn't a marshmallow like so many of the women he'd dated in the past.

Of course, he'd never dated Red. Maybe that was the problem. But he didn't think so. They'd bypassed the need to date almost immediately. There was no artifice between them. He didn't have to act like anyone except Tucker Alexander Gentry with her. And how freeing was that?

Yeah. He wanted to get a ring on her finger. He'd just have to work harder to convince her.

Monday, February 27 – Krewe of Orpheus Parade

When the knock came, Tag tried to ignore it. Red was in his bed. Naked, warm, pliable.

But the intruder didn't stop the rapping and even started calling through the door for Mr. Gentry or Ms. Schuyler.

Red groaned as Tag pulled away from her. He stepped into the sweatpants he'd left on the floor next to the bed.

"What?" he snapped as he opened the door.

"Delivery for Tucker Gentry and Celeste Schuyler."

"How did you even get back here?" Tag didn't care how cranky he sounded. No one should have disturbed the people in the guesthouse.

"Selena, the housekeeper, is my cousin's sister-in-law. She told me where to find you. I have your costumes for the masquerade tonight."

Tag echoed Red's groan. Then he hastily scrawled his name on the receipt. "Wait here," he grumbled. His wallet was on the bureau top. He extracted a five and handed it to the courier.

"What is it?" Red asked after the door was closed.

Tag stared at the two long boxes, one addressed to each of them. "Costumes for tonight."

Red shook her head. "I'm the caterer. I'll be in my chef whites."

"Nope. You're going to be my queen, remember?"

"Queen of the kitchen."

"Public proposal."

"Right."

They'd discussed the plan to death. She'd agreed to it. She didn't need to look so miserable about it.

Skye escaped the guesthouse as quickly as she could. She had too many last-minute details to attend to laze around in Tag's bed, as tempting as it might be.

She also booked their flights out of New Orleans for early the following morning. If she and Tag stayed in New Orleans, the remnants of her heart might not survive. Once she was home, she could cut him off. Isolate herself. Try to heal.

The costume someone had rented for her was a skeleton, much like the one that had so terrified her at the Krewe d'Etat parade. No way was she wearing that. Her chef whites were good enough. She wanted no mistake as to the woman Tag publicly asked to marry him. Her plan was as much for his protection as for hers.

The household was quiet, as if all the houseguests were resting to save their energy for one big burst of activity.

Her refuge was the kitchen.

Andouille gumbo simmered in a slow cooker and scented the kitchen with garlic and the distinctive aroma of filé. Pocket doors had been opened, turning most of the first floor of Noah's house into party central. Skye set up the buffet in the dining room. She was pleased with how everything looked. She'd done her best to make this ill-begotten party a success. If it failed, the food would not be at fault. She'd rolled shrimp jambalaya in purple and green cabbage leaves as a finger food. The diced bell pepper salad glistened in its dressing. Toothpicks speared the roasted fingerling potatoes, as if roasted potatoes were a common hors d'oeuvre.

She stood before the buffet table, hands on hips, more critical than anyone else could ever be. Stands of Mardi Gras-colored plastic beads slithered across the pure white tablecloth. The setup needed no other decor. The lighting in the dining room was brighter than in the designated party area.

She retreated to the kitchen when she heard the first of the revelers arrive.

It was going to be a long night.

Tag slipped into his costume. Looked in the mirror. Grimaced. Panels of yellow, green, and purple velvet formed a heavy robe. The mask looked heavy but wasn't. Still, it was an ugly looking thing, with a huge nose and a smarmy smile. The yellow crown was painted papier-mâché. The only good thing about the costume was the long scepter. Tag figured he could use it to replace the cane that had disappeared when the drunken frat boys had trashed his rental car.

Several hours later, Skye peeked into the dining room to see if she could clear away any empty platters or replenish others. It was nearly time to serve the king cake. She'd cut the pastry ring into thin slices. The plastic baby was safe in her pocket, ready to be inserted into the slice she served Tag.

One of the many costumed kings in attendance grabbed her wrist and pulled her into the dining room. Tag. Who else would know what she was up to?

Except it wasn't Tag.

"Look what I found," the masked king crowed.

Skye plastered on a smile and tried to pull free, but the grip on her arm was too strong to break without making a scene.

"I'll be serving the king cake in just a moment," she announced to cover the awkwardness of the situation. She hadn't felt this...threatened since Drake Dixon's Halloween party. But there was no reason for her to feel threatened.

Skye tried to locate Tag in the convergence of royalty. But there were too many dim corners, too many skeletons leering at her. Too damn many masks.

Noah was dressed as court jester. He'd abandoned his mask early, probably because it interfered with his drinking. Or so Skye guessed.

The masked king pulled Skye to Noah's side. That's when she spotted Tag. Yes, he was in one of the ubiquitous king costumes, but he leaned on his scepter instead of brandishing it the way some of the other kings were.

When he spotted her at Noah's side, he abruptly left a satin-swathed woman in a green-feathered mask.

"How's it going?" he asked as he approached.

The tightness in her chest eased when she recognized his voice.

"Okay. Quiet." She looked around the room. No obvious sex. Thank goodness Noah wasn't hosting an orgy.

Tag's gray eyes glittered silver through eyeholes in his mask. "Noah, let go of my queen."

Noah snorted. "This is Skye, not Terra."

"Terra is the kingdom whore, not my queen. Now unhand Red."

Definitely Tag. A sober and regal Tag.

Noah continued acting the fool.

Skye wrenched free of Noah's clammy hand. As much as she wanted to tell him to buzz off, her training wouldn't allow it. He was the customer. And unless he did something really bad, as Drake Dixon had done, Noah was right. The customer was always right.

"I need to serve the king cake," she reminded him.

"Right." The whiskey on his breath was sour.

Skye averted her face. "Come with me," she told Tag under her breath. "I'm going to give you the baby, which will make you the king of the party."

"You never did explain this to me," he said.

She purposely kept her pace slow so Tag could keep up.

"The king has to host the next party or purchase the next king cake. I have a spare cake you can provide for breakfast."

"Good to know."

When she was certain they were out of sight of the revelers, she palmed the plastic baby to Tag. "Remember, just stick this in your piece of cake, and don't choke on it."

The partygoers weren't going to miss this important Carnival tradition. Skye's face ached from smiling as she served the cake.

"I have the baby!" someone called out.

"No, I have the baby," a woman in red feathers said.

Several other people also claimed to have the baby.

Skye shook her head at Tag. He jerked his head just once.

Someone had sabotaged the king cake.

Noah scowled at her. She shrugged and lifted her hands, palms up, letting him know she had no idea what was going on. The cake had been unattended in the kitchen since she'd frosted it the previous day.

And Noah had dragged her away from the cut and plated slices just when she'd been about to serve. So someone had had ample opportunity to salt the cake with too many babies.

But why?

She found out a moment later. Someone grabbed her arm again. Pulled her away from the dining room. Into the kitchen. A king, but not Tag. This party was a stacked deck of royalty.

This person was a stranger or someone she hadn't bothered to note.

"What do you want?" she asked when he released her. She was going to have a map of bruises on her arm before she left New Orleans.

"A conversation." The king's voice was raspy. Deep. Familiar.

Chills erupted on her bruises.

"Why the baby boom?" She edged toward the stove, where the cast-iron skillet she'd used to brown the andouille still sat after she'd put it on a burner to dry after washing it.

"A minor distraction."

"Say your piece, then. I need to get back out there."

"You have to pay for what you did to me."

"Ah. Mr. Dixon." She spoke softly. "I thought I recognized your voice. The other night too. At the parade. You were a skeleton there, though."

The king laughed. "Believe what you will."

"You have your revenge. The entire baseball world thinks I blew Tag in to the press for using steroids. Isn't that payment enough? Although I fail to see why you think I've done anything to you. You were the one who tried to rape me."

"The video."

She shook her head. "Not me. Remember?" And that was true. The damning evidence of his Halloween attack on her was on Tag's cell phone, not hers. Of course, Tag had sent her a copy, which she'd uploaded to her website for storage, but Dixon didn't need to know that.

"You finally figured out a way to get back at me," Skye said. "There's not a professional sports team will hire me now."

Speaking to the clownish king mask was disconcerting, but she could imagine Dixon's smirk.

"A side benefit, to be sure."

"So you've ruined me. What else could you possible want from me?"

"What you didn't give me at Halloween."

She was careful not to lean against the stove as she slowly reached back. Her chef whites weren't flame retardant.

"You want to rape me?" He didn't scare her. Not like he had before.

"Seduce you."

"Sex is a power play with you. That makes it rape."

"You give it out for Gentry. Why not me? I have more money. I'm...able-bodied."

"She puts out for me because we're engaged," Tag said as he came into the kitchen. He'd removed his mask. His face was red and tufts of his damp hair stood upright. Perspiration trickled down the sides of his face.

"You? Married? Oh Terra is going to love that." Dixon started laughing.

Skye used the distraction to grab the skillet from the burner.

"I don't give a rat's ass what Terra thinks or how she feels. Except sorry. I'm going to make her very sorry for that fake news story about me and steroids."

"You can't prove anything."

"Neither could she, but she put her story out there anyway."

"You're just grasping at straws."

Tag lifted his right shoulder in a careless shrug. "Or getting ready to burn them."

Skye tightened her grip on the skillet.

"All I have to do," Tag continued, "is release the video of you threatening Red. I think people will question the motivation behind her stolen phone. Behind Terra's sudden scoop. Especially since you talk about Terra in the video. And not in very flattering terms either."

How did Tag remember that? Skye had few memories of that night other than terror followed by relief. She hadn't listened to her instincts back then. Unlike this sojourn in New Orleans. For all the good it had done her.

The smooth iron handle of the skillet felt right against her palm. Comfortable.

"You were the one with your dick hanging out, not me," Tag reminded Dixon. "Threatening a woman and a man in a wheelchair. Who do you think will come out on top of that one?"

"I'll sue." Dixon's voice trembled ever so slightly.

Tag's laugh sounded more like a bark. "For what? Sneaking a cell phone into your orgy? The damage is done, Dixon. You decided to ignore the ground rules I laid down. Now you have to pay the consequences."

That was when Skye noticed Dixon's scepter. It wasn't at all like Tag's, who was using his as a cane.

In fact, Dixon's scepter looked suspiciously like the cane that had been stolen from Tag's rental car, right down to the distinctive teal pinstriping on the black matte finish. The detailing wouldn't have been noticed in the dim light of the party. Pretty nervy move on Dixon's part.

Dixon didn't raise his scepter but kept it low. Some instinct screamed in Skye's ear, and she grasped the skillet with both hands and swung it like a bat at the same moment Dixon went for Tag's game leg. The cast iron connected with the cane.

Skye felt the contact reverberation in her arms. Dixon howled his frustration and tried to swing again, but the element of surprise was gone, and Tag evaded the blow.

Skye screamed and swung again. This time, the skillet connected with Dixon's fingers, smashing them against the granite of the island. His howl turned into a shriek that muffled the sound of the cane clattering to the tile floor.

Terra and Noah pushed into the kitchen. "What's going on?" Noah asked. "Who's screaming?"

Skye held her skillet in front of her chest like a shield.

"Dixon's up to his usual tricks," Tag said.

"She attacked me with her frying pan!"

Noah's face blanched.

"You attacked Tag first." Skye was amazed her voice was so calm, so steady. Her insides quivered like tomato aspic. "Call the police."

"Wait a minute." Noah sounded more nervous than she did. "No need for police for a…disagreement."

"Assault," Skye retorted. "Attempted rape. I'm pressing charges." Oh it felt so good to say those words.

"Call an ambulance. The bitch broke my hand." Dixon cradled his hand against his abdomen.

"I'll drive you to the ER." Noah nearly stuttered the words.

"You're drunk," Dixon replied.

"No one is driving anywhere," Terra said. "Not tonight. Not through the crowds on the street. An ambulance is your best bet."

Tag had worked his way across the kitchen until he stood next to Skye. "I want the cops." His tone was as flat and hard as the bottom of the skillet. "I'm tired of Dixon's games. I'm tired of the threats. Our *gentlemen's* agreement was he would leave Red alone, and we wouldn't report his attempted assault on her. He broke his part of the bargain."

"You can't prove anything." Dixon snarled. "Who's going to believe a washed-up ball player and his fuck buddy?"

Skye flinched at the description, then owned it. That's what she was. Strength came in truth.

"Don't talk about my fiancée that way. And yeah, we have proof. We have the Halloween video."

"Fiancée?" Terra's tone rivaled the blade on Skye's boning knife. "You still want to marry her?"

"Yes." Tag didn't look at Terra. Didn't look at anyone except Skye. In the eyes. Intently. As if he meant what he was saying.

"After she exposed your steroid usage?" Terra's outrage sounded almost real.

Tag brushed a stray strand of hair from Skye's cheek. She tried not to flinch, tried to gaze at him with the same adoration with which he gazed at her.

"You forget, Terra. I was there when you gave Red's phone back to her. She didn't have her phone in her possession when the e-mail was sent to you. Date stamps. Remember? Nice try, though. I'm surprised at the lengths you went to salvage a relationship that never existed."

"That's not true." Terra didn't sound as upset as Skye would have been in her position. "I love you."

Skye couldn't help herself. She burst out laughing.

"What's so funny?" Noah asked. "Terra has always loved Tag. Everybody knows it."

Skye wiped the dampness from her eyes. "She sure has a funny way of showing it. I really wouldn't want to be on her shit list."

Tag's grin was lopsided as he pulled out his cell phone.

"Wait." Noah lurched for the phone, but he was unsteady on his feet. "Don't call the cops."

Skye could almost smell the desperation rising off him like miasma from a grave.

"Terra didn't steal Skye's phone or take the photo to send to herself. I did. It was a joke. I didn't know she'd actually file a story about it. You know me. A joker." He indicated his costume. "The court jester."

Tag's face twisted into a sneer. "Nobody's laughing."

Noah glanced at Dixon, then tried again. "No cops. The party just got a little out of hand. It's a *party*. That's what happens. It's Mardi Gras. The French Quarter. You take your chances."

Weariness slammed into Skye. She'd wanted to leave for so many days, but everything had thwarted that plan. There was nothing more Dixon or anyone could do. The party was over. She toed Tag's cane, now bent and useless. "Looks like I owe you a new cane. Can we get out of here?"

"Are you sure?"

"Dixon got to threaten me again. I ought to be used to that by now. I catered the stupid party. It really is time for me to leave."

Tag glared at Dixon. "Leave us alone. Tell your flunkies—Noah, Terra, Tripp Shaneybrook—tell them all to leave us alone. Last warning, or you're really not going to like our damage control."

Tuesday, February 28 – Mardi Gras

R ed's friendship with her cab driver turned out to be one of the best parts of Tag's trip to New Orleans. Kahil picked them up bright and early and drove them to the airport.

There were no good-byes to Noah or his guests.

Despite the long wait before their flight, Tag agreed with Red that hanging at the airport was better than being at Noah's place.

"*I'm probably gonna get sued for this,*" a familiar voice intoned over one of the televisions annoyingly mounted and blaring everywhere. "*I can't discuss my patients.*"

Hector Michaud, physical therapist extraordinaire, was being ambushed by a ballsy reporter.

"*You worked with him every day he's been in New Orleans,*" the reporter probed.

"*I'm not going to risk losing my license over idle gossip,*" Hector snapped.

"*Can you comment on his injuries?*"

Hector kept walking.

Tag recognized the parking lot of Hector's building.

Hector stopped. Turned. Faced the camera. "*I run an honest practice. It is the policy of my practice to promote healing in the most natural ways possible. I won't work with anyone trying to game the system.*"

The SUV behind him chirped. He opened the door, climbed in, and drove away. The reporter went into a recap of the nonstory.

Red looked at Tag. "What is that supposed to mean?"

Tag shrugged. "I guess it's why I had to pee in a cup at every visit."

Red's eyes widened. "You have proof you weren't doping?"

"Medical records. Confidential."

"Can't you release them yourself?"

He shook his head. "I could, but I would also have to release my physical condition and the extent of my injury. Not sure I'm ready to do that yet."

He doubted he would ever be ready. A sour ball of fear pummeled his stomach. He wasn't ready to give up baseball. He was going to beat this injury. Maybe he could convince Hector to move to Columbia.

"Hi, there." Chelsea and Tripp Shaneybrook ambled into the restaurant where Tag and Red were sipping coffee, waiting for their flight. "Can we join you?" Shaneybrook asked.

Tag didn't want anyone's company except Red's, but she was smiling and nodding at the Shaneybrooks, so it looked as if he wasn't going to get his way.

"Are you sure you want to sit with someone who's a doper?" Tag couldn't keep the sneer out of his voice.

"I don't think you are. You have too much respect for the game and for your body," Shaneybrook replied.

"Congratulations on your engagement," his wife said.

"Thanks," Tag said, before Red could deny the story.

"Had a long talk with Noah this morning," Shaneybrook said.

Tag couldn't care less. Noah Nash was definitely off his Christmas card list.

"Guys!" Red clutched Tag's arm and pointed to the television. "Look."

A reporter was doing a stand-up outside Noah's house.

Breaking news.

Tag yawned and sat up.

Drake Dixon and Noah Nash were being led from the house by police. Both men were handcuffed.

"What the—"

"Drake Dixon and former Columbia Gems' pitcher Noah Nash were taken into custody a short time ago," the reporter explained. *"Charges of illegal gambling, including bets placed on baseball games, are pending. Dixon is the majority shareholder of the Columbia Gems. The two men have been arrested following several months of investigations by the FBI—"*

Tag blocked out the rest of the reporter's spiel.

Gambling. On baseball.

"Is that bad?" Red asked.

"Ever hear of a guy named Pete Rose?" Tag responded.

"It's bad." Shaneybrook sounded grim.

Tag swallowed the last of his coffee. "Do you suppose Noah was going to ask me to throw baseball games?"

"You wouldn't have done it," Red said. "So it's a moot point."

Her faith in him filled him with wonder. Her loyalty somehow made him a better man. He grabbed her hand. "I really like having you on my team. I think I need to put a no-trade clause in your contract."

"You have to get me to sign, first." She smiled at him. A little flirtatious. Maybe for the Shaneybrooks' benefit. Or maybe for real.

"I thought you two were already engaged," Chelsea said. "Or did I miss something?"

"Negotiations are on-going," Tag said. "But I'm confident."

"Arrogant," Red said. But she was still smiling.

Her smiles stole his breath. "And you love it."

Something flashed in her eyes. If he hadn't been watching her so closely, he might have missed it. He never wanted to miss anything about her. That meant keeping her close. Not a hardship.

"Have your agent call me." Her smile had faded. But she was still looking at him. That had to mean something.

"Nah. This is one acquisition I'm handling on my own."

I hope you enjoyed this installment of Tag and Skye's story.

For up-to-date information about my books, please sign up for my newsletter.

EXCERPT: CATCHER INTERFERENCE (TAG & SKYE PART 1)

October 20, Game 7 National League Championship Series

Tucker Alexander Gentry, known throughout the baseball universe as Tag, squatted behind home plate. His thigh muscles burned. He glared at the pitcher on the mound.

The entire season had come down to this moment. Game seven of the National League Championship Series. Top of the ninth inning. Two outs. The Columbia Gems were up by one, and Tag meant to keep the score that way. The tying run was on second base—some cocky wiseass New York had recently called up from Triple-A for the postseason. The go-ahead run was on first.

And Adam Chrestler, the Gems' closing pitcher, was shaking off Tag's signals. The oversize digital scoreboard played stupid cartoon graphics behind Chrestler's head. The ballpark was so silent Tag thought he heard the hot dog vendor on the third-base side of the stadium scouring his grill.

Tag thrust his hand between his splayed thighs and flashed the sign for a slider. *Do not pitch a fastball.* Chrestler's slider was working. And the batter at the plate could knock a fastball out of the park.

If that happened, the Gems would hang up their cleats until spring. If not, the team would go to the World Series. Only one out away.

Don't think ahead. One game at a time.

If Chrestler threw a fastball, Tag would personally break a couple of the pitcher's fingers.

Chrestler released the ball. The hitter swung. The bat met the ball—loud as a firecracker—but not with the distinctive sound only made by the sweet spot on a maple bat connecting with cowhide. The batter had gotten under the pitch. Long fly ball. Leisurely sailing toward right field. The sole shooting star against the black backdrop of the nighttime sky.

The right fielder adjusted his cup and positioned his body for the catch. The play should have resulted in an easy out, but the ball smacked his glove before it bobbled to the grass.

The fans groaned, but Tag barely heard them. He focused on the punk who tagged up at second and headed for third. Tag threw off his mask and readied himself to protect home plate. Yep. The New York third-base coach was waving the punk home.

Shit, he was fast.

Tag stood directly behind the plate, silently cursing the rule change that prevented him from blocking the base. He wasn't taking any chances the out would be overturned because he'd messed up. Because he was going to make the out. Ensure his team would go to the World Series.

The ball rocketed in from right field. Punk's teeth flashed in a cocky grin the second before he went into his slide.

Tag stretched himself to catch the ball that was zooming toward him. The punk was sliding. Dust and chalk from the base path were like a jet contrail pluming behind him.

The ball landed in Tag's mitt, stinging his palm ever so slightly. He lunged forward, twisted ever so slightly, and tagged Punk's foot before it touched the base. The ump called the out.

Punk's cleats connected with the back of Tag's right knee where his leg guards didn't cover. Retracted ever so slightly, and then slammed the spot anew with the full force of Punk's body behind it.

It didn't matter. The game was over. The Columbia Gems had won the National League Pennant and were World Series bound.

Tag's teammates burst from the dugout and jumped him. Pounded his back. Danced around home plate. Fireworks exploded in the no-man's land behind the scoreboard, and a sulfuric stench from the gunpowder wafted into the stadium.

Tag's throat was dry from the billowing dust and all the whooping. He couldn't wait to get into the clubhouse and pop open the champagne management had on ice for just this occasion. It was sure going to taste mighty fine.

His teammates finally decided to let him up. He tried to stand.

His first clue something was wrong was the way his right leg wouldn't support him. The second indication was the pain that stole his breath and a sense of wetness. He hadn't been doused with the water bucket—that honor was reserved for the manager—so he looked down. And nearly puked.

EXCERPT: BATTING CLEAN UP (Tag & Skye Part 3)

Wednesday, March 1

"You're not Jewish?" Joel Green, the new director of Columbia's Jewish Community Center, eyed Celeste "Skye" Schuyler with suspicion.

"Nope." Skye forced her cheeriness. "But I do have my kosher certification. I explained all this to your predecessor when he signed the contract for me to cater the Purim Carnival."

She kept her smile firmly in place. Didn't even grit her teeth.

"Kosher is more than no lobster or bacon." The poor man was truly distressed.

"I know. Don't worry. My certification is legitimate. And I'm a vegan caterer, too. The two cuisines work well together."

He didn't seem assured. "Why would you cater kosher meals if you're not Jewish?"

"I like to cook. I like studying various cuisines. I saw a need for a kosher caterer in Columbia. It was a business decision."

She didn't know what her religious or cultural orientation had to do with her ability to cook kosher. Yes, she understood *kashrut*—the dietary laws—wasn't the same as being able to cook Thai or French. But the secondary kitchen in her Skye's The Limit building had been certified kosher. She had completely separate cooking utensils. She understood what she could and couldn't do. In fact, she'd already catered a wedding reception at one of the local synagogues. Her credentials had been scrutinized by the previous director of the JCC before he signed the contract for her to cater the Purim Carnival.

Green finally smiled at her, but the ice in his vivid blue eyes didn't melt. "Given the current political climate, you have to understand why the center is being cautious."

She'd heard about the rise in hate crimes around the country. She couldn't escape it. Especially when she was a victim, too.

"Nothing has happened here, has it?" she asked.

"There was a threat back in January. And the Purim Carnival is the first big event we've had this calendar year, so it's...attractive. We'll be beefing up security as well as taking a closer look at all our vendors."

He was trying to tell her his questions weren't personal. "Completely understandable."

Skye really needed this job. She'd signed the contract the previous autumn, right after her certification had come through. She'd been scrambling then, trying to come up with a balloon payment on her mortgage. Then the local baseball team won the National League pennant and went to the World Series. Since her contract with the Columbia Gems called for her to cater all home games, she'd gotten four unexpected but quite welcome jobs from the series.

Catering jobs weren't the only thing she'd gotten.

"And frankly, something came up in our background check on you that concerns us."

Skye's stomach dropped, probably along with her blood pressure. She knew what was coming.

"Tag Gentry," Green said.

Tag Gentry. The Columbia Gems catcher whose play at the plate during the final game of the National League pennant race had put the Gems in the World Series. Who'd sacrificed his leg for his team. Who had become Skye's friend with benefits when the team hired her to feed him during his initial rehab. Who she'd had the complete lack of common sense to fall in love with.

Yeah. That guy.

ALSO BY MJ COMPTON

CONTEMPORARY SPORTS (BASEBALL) ROMANCE

COLUMBIA GEMS BASEBALL ROMANCES

MISSING THE SIGNS – A second chance with the sexy baseball player who ghosted me seven years ago? Let me count the "no ways".

HIT BY HIS PITCH – I was abandoned. Stranded. Broke. Until the playboy pitcher came in for the save.

CATCHER INTERFERENCE: TAG & SKYE PART 1 – One injured catcher. One sizzling caterer. A torrid post-season game neither can afford to lose.

NO DOUBLES DEFENSE: TAG & SKYE PART 2 – What's an injured catcher to do when spring training starts without him? Losing himself in the decadence of Mardi Gras seems like a good start.

BATTING CLEANUP: TAG & SKYE PART 3 – Baseball may be the only place in life where a sacrifice is really appreciated, but catcher Tag Gentry never expected Skye Schuyler to risk everything for him.

SHIFTER- BASEBALL MASHUP NOVELLA

Shifting Home – The only shift baseball star Spike Peters knows is when players realign their defensive positions on the field. But when the most attractive woman he's ever encountered starts babbling about shifting, full moons, fated mates, and—worst of all—forever, the fastest runner in the game's first instinct is to run—straight to her bed.

SHIFTER ROMANCE

Toke Lobo & the Pack Series

MOONLIGHT SERENADE-Werewolves working for the government? Reporter Delilah Tenney must choose:the story of a lifetime or a lifetime of love.

"Compton's debut is a gripping, sexy as hell, page turner of a were-wolf novel not for the faint hearted!" ~ NY Times Bestselling Author Maggie Shayne.

AND JERICHO BURNED- Lucy Callahan will do anything to save her sister, even if that means marrying a stranger. Even if that stranger is an undercover government agent out to destroy the cult holding her sister hostage. Even if that stranger is a . . . werewolf.

A Night Owl Reviews Reviewer Top Choice.

OMEGA MOON RISING- One desperate woman intent on escape. One brash werewolf determined to deny his DNA. Until his destiny becomes her deliverance.

A Night Owl Reviews Reviewer Top Choice.

Service for Sanctuary Series

BETRAYED BY THE MOON – Service for sanctuary–that was the werewolves' deal for over 200 years. Now the government is changing the rules, leaving Ethan Calhoun fighting for the only way of life he's ever known— and Selena Wolfe fighting for her life.

BEWARE OF THE MOON – One-night stands don't turn into forever unless you happen to pick-up a werewolf. She thought the hook-up was just another one-and-done. He knew she was his one-and-only. But when his mission unlocks the treacheries of her past, they are forced to put aside their differences as they battle for their lives.

BESIEGED BY THE MOON – Fated soul mates. She's a werewolf assassin in heat on a mission. He's a werewolf EMT and the father of her future children. What could possibly go wrong?

About the Author

MJ Compton grew up near Cardiff, New York, a place best known for its giant—a hoax so successful, P.T. Barnum duplicated it. The tale of the "petrified man" convinced MJ that inventing stories could be a career.

Although her 30 years working in local television included such highlights as being bitten by a lion, preempting a US President for a college basketball game, giving a three-time world champion boxer a few black eyes, and meeting her husband, MJ never lost her dream of creating her own stories.

MJ still lives in upstate New York with her husband. Music and cooking are two of her passions, and she enjoys baseball, college basketball, and sitting on her patio on summer nights to count lightning bugs, but she's primarily focused on writing.